Mike,

Thanks For all The

Best morning shows
And laughs! And
pushing The interesting
"Tales" of mart.

Enjoy This Tale ...
Sequel June 2024

B. Diamonds

Tales

OF THE

Knights

#1

OVER THE HORIZON

MMXXIII

Hot Armor Press

REVISED EDITION
COPYRIGHT 2024

Diamond/DiAngelo
MUSIC & BOOKS
WORLDWIDE

EDITED AND FORMATTED BY

R. H. BAUDERER
EDITOR

COVER - RoCaCola

TALES OF THE KNIGHTS
"OVER THE HORIZON"

... is dedicated to all of YOU who have supported me.

Your words of encouragement inspire me to keep telling my stories. I may never be a rich man but I will forever BE enriched, knowing that you have enjoyed these Tales.

Thank you to Robert H. Bauderer for all the HARD work of content editing, formatting and contributions; and of course Rodney DiAngelo for cover design, marketing and co-publishing.

To my loving MUTTER, who is the ROCK of our Family, and to Brittany, Sabrina, Angelo, Abella, Ari, Coyote, and those still to come.

And as ALWAYS ... I Thank God for giving me this gift of creativity; and to be able to share it with you ...

May the Good Lord Bless You!

B. Diamond

TALES

OF THE

KNIGHTS

OVER THE HORIZON

The fear was clear in her young eyes as those who were sworn to protect her fall around her like saplings trampled by herds of oxen. The hordes of Norsemen had but one objective; the Lady Chastity of the Norse. The Lady was once betrothed to Víðarr the Vicious by her father Týr, a former Norse tribal leader. When she was only twelve, Chastity's beauty had already captured the eyes of the dominate tribal leader, Víðarr of the far north.

Being the age of thirty years, Víðarr agreed to give Týr and his people peace, and allow them to live without the fear of being slaughtered, like so many other small tribes. Of course this would be for a price … or should it be said, a 'prize'.

A few months before Chastity was to be wed at the age of seventeen, Týr fled to Britain with his clan, who had now converted to the new religion; Christianity. Víðarr had no use for Christians, except to plunder, as he had already done along the Irish coast.

Víðarr considered these, "Christians" and their monks and priests easy prey, and he took whatever their places of worship held. Having killed many defenseless holy men, he had taken their treasures from them, to feed his horde.

This had gained him an army that baptized in blood those who opposed his deadly vicious rule.

Víðarr had high paid spies that informed him of the whereabouts of his seventeen year old bride to be. Finally a Bishop, who had been paid off, told Víðarr the whereabouts of a small castle which was entrusted to Týr and his small clan. It was located just a half day ride from the coast.

Týr had no more than one hundred men to defend this small castle, so the overwhelming force of a thousand warriors would not take long to slaughter them all, and Víðarr would bring his *prize* back with him.

Týrs only hope was a Knight that he had befriended after arriving in England.

Just months before ... Chastity had fallen into a raging flooded river after a violent storm.

Suddenly out of nowhere, a Knight on a horse as white as virgin snow appeared. Having shed his armor and weaponry in a flash, he dove into the frigid waters and pulled Chastity to the shore. Ten years older than the Lady, the Knight, Robert Goldheart, was also captivated by the beauty before him.

Týr offered a great reward for the rescue, but Robert replied, "I cannot take a reward for this, as this was caused by the Mother of Nature. But if ever you need the service of protection from the evils of man ... then we shall discuss a reward."

Robert was the second son of a man who was the primary keeper and maker of the Kings gold decor. But upon his father's death, the estate, as tradition would have it, went to the eldest son; his brother Edward.

But Robert didn't care, for on that fateful day on the river, Robert received something more meaningful to him than all his brothers riches could ever buy, a very quick but affectionate kiss.

PART 2

Chastity closes her eyes in prayer with every blow of death that she sees from above in her tower. Her father looks up at her and knows that Víðarr intends to kill all for what he and his loyal Norsemen have come to collect. Týrs hopes that the message that he has sent with a young soldier, gets to the brave Knight Robert Goldheart in time. He had always offered to save the one thing so many have died for, and continue to die for … Lady Chastity of the Norse.

As most of Týrs clan are taking their last breath, he gives the orders to open the castle gate. Thirty more charge out into the overwhelming odds, as the young Lady contemplates using the dagger on her side on herself. Chastity grabs a crucifix with one hand, and drops to her knees.

*"Lord Christ, I am a new convert, and wish to never to be in the arms of Víðarr. I know if I pray things will be as they should be. But please forgive me oh Merciful One, as I am weak. I cannot, and will not submit to a man suited for Satan. I pray, as I look **over the horizon**, with all of my heart, and my belief in you, that there is another way ... Amen."*

As she finishes her prayer, thirty former Norse riders, who have been trained in the tactics of the west, ride toward the bloodbath before them. They know that soon, they too, shall be within the carnage which bloodies the once life giving soil.

Their lances are lowered in unison; the thirty in line, charge at full speed without fear, yet all know that these may be their last moments upon this earth.

From above, Chastity observes, watching the last charge of her homeland Norse tribe.

Clutching the sheath by her side, her young hands grab the handle. If her prayer to the new religion does not materialize, it would soon be time to withdraw the weapon.

Closing her eyes, she suddenly feels warmth. The same warmth she had felt that cold river day. Looking down, she sees more than three hundred Knights from the left and the right, joining her father's charge toward the intruders. Looking toward the heavens, Chastity speaks loudly, "Praise be to the Lord Jesus!"

At the forefront of the charge, Chastity sees a brave Knight upon his stallion. A Knight that once held her close, but wished that he could have held her closer.

Watching the English Knights mow down the intruders from the across the sea, Chastity gives thanks to her new faith. Her heart is relieved to see her father and fifty men still alive. But her heart and soul search for only one. He is covered in blood, and out of breath, but still alive.

That evening, a celebration was held inside the small castle as word had reached all ...
"The evil Norsemen have sailed back home."

Týr was relieved, and offered Robert a nobleman's ransom. But the Knight had only those that rode with him in mind. He took just what they needed; far less than what was offered.

With the celebration going on inside the small castle, Robert sits outside by a campfire. He knows in his heart, that the young woman he once rescued is of Norse royalty, and therefore she may only marry a Noble Norseman.

He watches the golden sun slowly fade **over the horizon** ... deep in thought of what he knows could never be. But in all his years, he knows, his heart has never been lost to a Lady as it now is to this Lady of the Norse...

Robert Goldheart already knows that there will be no other that his heart could ever belong to.

Týr finishes paying the brave Knights that saved him, and what is left of his clan, from total annihilation. Týr now wishes to reward one more, for again saving all he and others are willing to die for.

Walking to the fire, Týr offers Robert a leather bag filled with silver. Robert kneels before him, "Oh great Norse leader, I am humbled before you, and ask only that I am given the chance to earn the Lady Chastity's affections. I truly know in my heart that all I love, and all I shall ever seek, will never be **over the horizon**, but always in my mind and heart … with the visions of the Lady Chastity".

Týr stands stone faced before the kneeling Knight wishing to grasp his head with his hand and give his blessings. But he cannot. He has already made another arrangement with a rich powerful Noble in this new land. Within these new terms, Týr and his remaining clan and castle will be under the protection of this man.

A father has again bequeathed his daughter for the good of all to survive. He tells the Knight that the promised husband is one called Edward Goldheart … the brother of Robert.

Wanting to rise in anger and hurt, Robert stays kneeled and wonders how his brother, who is twice widowed, may have even learned of Lady Chastity of the Norse.

There is only one person that he told of how he felt, and about the beauty of the Lady … the Bishop of London … during a confession. He knows that the Bishop is also a confidant to his brother Edward.

Once again, his brother is taking something that Robert holds dear. But this time it's the most precious thing of all. He knows that what a person tells a priest in confession should have gone no further, and for that alone … the Bishop will someday pay.

Týr sees the hurt in this man's face, "I can tell you have love for my daughter. As a man who knows this look, I do understand. But what I do, I do for those within these walls. Many of them are without fathers, husbands, sons, or brothers. I owe you the greatest of debts for our survival ... but you do not have the same power or guarantees as your brother Edward. I am compelled to give you something that to you will be worth more than all the silver I still have. I will grant permission to keep company with my daughter, in the tower from the first breath of morning's sun, until the last glimmer of its farewell shine. You will be observed by Agnes the Old. She will not be close, but also not far. Make the best of your time ... but know that there will never be more. I spare you one thing ... the pain of having someone so deep within your heart, and knowing she is forever gone. The feeling I endure every day. Only we will ever know of this, it is all I can give. With the rooster's crow your time starts, with the owls hoot, it will end."

Týr turns and walks away ... wishing what he could do ... but knowing what he *must* do.

Walking to the stables, Robert approaches his trusted steed, one he calls, Pegasus. Seeing a slight wound which has already been tended to with ointment ... he looks into the eyes of his four legged friend, "Well, it looks like after tomorrow, you will be the only one to give me your affections. You are a masterful steed Pegasus, God willing, some day we fall together."

A big burly voice interrupts the caring moment, "You were not granted the Lady Chastity's hand, and come to get comfort from your stallion?"

Turning around and looking up, a man, a head and a half taller, with shiny baldness is smiling down at him. Knowing that the man is just trying to lighten the moment, Robert responds, "Henry, I am not in a place of joy right now, I know you mean well, but this time I feel as if my heart has been eaten out by a flock of ravens."

Henry the Bald, as he is called, is a massive man who bears and swings a sword that most men cannot even lift. He is the youngest cousin of Robert's mother, who on her death bed, vowed to forever take Robert under his care, as Edward was always under his father's affectionate eyes.

The big massive hand touches Roberts shoulder, "Come, I have persuaded a monk to part with a keg of his finest ale for just two Holy Land coins."

Robert smiles, "No my big friend, tonight it is all yours, but perhaps after sunset tomorrow, I will be needing a great amount of ale to numb the place within my chest that once held a heart."

The big hand gives Robert a slight pat, knocking him forward, "Yes, then I will make sure this keg is good tonight, and get another one for two more Roman coins tomorrow."

Robert shakes his head, "Henry, those coins you have bear the likeness of an Emperor of Rome, before the Lord Jesus was ever born."

"Besides they were minted in Rome, not in Jerusalem. They were likely never there in the Holy land."

Henry gives Robert a wink, "You said *likely*, so you don't know, and neither do I. But the monk believes it so, and who am I to interfere with a monks beliefs?"

Henry walks away singing an Old Norse drinking tune as Robert turns and begins to give Pegasus a handful of grain. Suddenly a noise behind him makes Robert think that Henry must not have grabbed his drinking tankard. Not turning around Robert says, "Henry, why not just open the wooden spout on the keg while holding it over your head. That way you may only need a few drinks before the keg is empty."

A pause of silence, then a sweet soft voice responds, "Oh Lord, can Henry the Bald do that?"

Turning quickly, Robert sees what has taken his heart. "Lady Chastity, I … I thought … I mean I was told our day would start tomorrow and that…"

Chastity puts her hand over Roberts lips, "Robert, please be silent and listen, for I have not much time. Take me away; I know the love I feel in my heart shall never be given to another. My father told me of what must be, and the day he has granted us. We can leave now … ride away and forever be within each other's arms. I love you and…"

Now Robert puts his hand over the lips he forever wishes to kiss, "My Lady, we cannot. To do so would disrespect your father, your clan, me … but most of all … you. Know this … for all the days that the Lord grants me, I will never love another but you my Lady. We have tomorrow together, and that must last me my lifetime. You must go now before other eyes see what only so few know. I love you Lady Chastity of the Norse, today, tomorrow and forever."

Chastity knows it must be so as well, and that she has to give up what she so loves.

Looking into the loving eyes of the Knight, she speaks, "You are a good man Robert Goldheart; I will be waiting to spend our life from the first twinkle of days light. You honor your crest well." Giving Robert a quick kiss, the Knight's heart feels it's as high as in heaven, yet as low as in hell.

Part 3

Before the roosters first crow, Robert walks toward the dimly lit towers entrance. Taking a step inside, the Knight is abruptly hit with a broom handle coming from an old face, bearing no emotion. "You! Stand outside until your time begins!!!"

Looking into her demanding eyes, he realizes that this old face must belong to Agnes the Old, who Týr had mentioned. She would keep a watchful eye throughout the time two hearts will spend their lifetime together.

Within a few moments, the rooster crows and the first rays from the eastern horizon bring a shine upon two silver chalices on a table.

"Enter Sir Robert Goldheart, the Lady Chastity awaits you on the terrace overlooking the eastern sunrise. But I must warn you ... if at any time during this visit, you break your vow of chivalry, I will and I can throw your Knights' rear end out of here, do we have an understanding?"

The forcefulness of this older woman almost makes Robert smile, but he knows best, "Yes Lady Agnes, I understand, you have my word."

Agnes hits Robert again with the broom handle, "I am Agnes the Old, not any velvet Lady. You have already wasted a minute of your time, go!"

Sitting on a bench made for two, Chastity's smile and eyes are aglow, and bring the same response from the face of a Knight.

Robert sits down next to the one he loves and Chastity's soft hand immediately interlocks with the rougher hand of the man that has taken her heart.

Before any words can even be spoken, a loud, **"Thump!"** is heard at a table a short distance away and behind the two.

Chastity whispers, "That's Agnes's way of letting us know she is watching." The two get a brief smile as they know, what just came up **over the horizon** in the east; will too soon set down **over the horizon** in the west.

At first it was awkward when way they both began to talk, but within an hour, the two were in conversation as if they had known each other for a lifetime. Chastity told Robert about Agnes, the woman who first looked after her mother at a young age, and then after her with her mother's death, when she was only five. Agnes the Old had always been with her and had always had the same look upon her face.

Glancing back at the watching eyes, Robert looks at his love, "You mean **that** same look? She appears as if ready to slay the devil himself!"

Chastity giggles a bit, "Yes, for the most part she always has that look. But don't let it frighten you my brave Knight, under that glare Agnes carries a good heart."

Robert can't resist, "Yes my Lady, but who's heart has she removed?"

Getting a slight slap on the arm, the two again laugh. A servant brought out a bite of food and a bottle of fine wine from the nearby monastery. Both Lady and Knight enjoyed their mid-day meal and were again holding each other's hand with loving tenderness in their hearts. With the mid-day shadows before them, the bench was turned toward the suns last hours. Both knew they must absorb every second of their last hours that will hopefully last them both a lifetime.

The conversation slows as the soft touch and tender stroke of a finger within the holding hands say more than any words ever could.

A final meal was offered, but the two hearts only hungered for what they could never again have. The shadows behind them seem to be growing now at record speed, as both sets of eyes look westward. Suddenly, the same as in the morning, a loud **"Thump!"** is heard.

The two turn to see Agnes still watching, "I have sat here and watched you two all day. I now must find a chamber pot. I will be gone the time it takes to boil an egg, and I will be unable to watch with my eyes. Make an everlasting time of what I cannot see or report."

Chastity looks at Agnes the Old. Her lips move but no words are spoken, "thank you".

Both watch as Agnes turns and slowly walks away.

Chastity turns toward the Knights confusion, "Kiss me you brave fool!"

Their lips passionately entangle with the love they share. Both hearts and minds in the place that they so wish for, but yet know it can never be.

In this enchanted moment, both dream of a wedding night together and what their love could have been like. Both minds lost in a love so pure that neither wants to come back to reality. The sound of a distant sneeze bring both out of their passionate loving embrace, but not before a last split second loving last kiss.

The sun is now sinking as if the hand of God is waving farewell. Tears begin to flow from the Lady's eyes as the Knight has a lump in his throat the size of an oxen's hoof.

A candle is lit behind them as a soft voice speaks out, "It is time Sir Knight. You may embrace the Lady for a few drips of candle wax, and then you must go ... forever."

The two stand and embrace, both know this is what must be. Both hearts have been filled with so much joy, and now both hearts are terminally broken. Robert looks into the beautiful eyes, now full of sorrow, "I will forever love you Lady Chastity of the Norse. In this world, and also in the next. Look for me there, as I will always be searching for you ...eternally"

Chastity, with tears running down her cheeks can only muster out, "I love you, and I will never stop. Always and forever."

Agnes clears her throat, a signal that their time is up, their gift has been given, but now their lives must part. Robert slowly lets go of what he never wished to release, while two sets of watery eyes take a final glance.

He walks toward the exit like a wounded warrior at heaven's gate. Agnes meets him there, "You are a good man Robert Goldheart. I so wish for you and the Lady that things would not so be."

Handing something to Robert, "Take this, for if ever the Lady is in your need, she will send for you, and you will know it's from her." Agnes places the item in Roberts hand and it is tenderly closed.

Looking at the once stone cold face, Robert can see in the old woman's eyes that she too feels pain for the two that can never be as one. "Agnes, I swear I will always be on a Knight's call for Lady Chastity of the Norse, no matter what her needs, I so swear it before you and before God."

Entering the stable, the moons glow illuminates the interior through the open portholes. Waking up to the only living thing he can tell his feelings to, and never be betrayed ...

Robert lets loose on the waiting large ears of his four legged friend. While tears flow, a long faced nose nuzzles close to his grieving friend.

After a few moments of words, spoken to an affectionate steed, a deep voice from another stable speaks up, "She must be very special, … for never have I seen you in so much pain, … with the exception of when you were a young lad at your dear mother's burial. Come my friend, we get ready to go."

Robert can see the moons light gleaming off the head of Henry the Bald, "Henry, I feel not like drinking. I am sure you can drink my portion and then some. I feel like …"

Henry interrupts, "Riding as fast and as far as you can. Yes I knew that is what would be. I am ready to go, your stead has been given grain and water, saddle him and we shall ride north. I have heard a nobleman is having problems with a band of Gaelic rebels and is willing to pay a handsome price of silver."

"It will be you and I and twelve loyal fighters, but not the King's Knights, for they have been called back by the King. We ride until we can ride no more, than I have a few small casks of wine that we must drink once opened."

Robert's broken heart is soothed by the words of his long-time companion. The Knight also knows that only a good entanglement with a foe will temperately take away the hurt that so burns within.

In a tower high above, a Lady watches the moon, the likes of which has not been seen in a lifetime, is rising. It is a moon that troubadours will venerate in their tunes of love as they travel from town to town.

The distraught Lady is feeling the loneliness within her as if she was all alone on that glorious moon. An old loving face sits down beside her, "My child, I cannot know what you feel as it has been two lifetimes since Víðarr's father slayed my only husband to be. I remember the pain. It has faded, but I will never forget the love I once had. Yes I had many a suitor while still young, but my heart could never love another. I know why you grieve, and who you grieve for. This new religion called Christianity, talks of peace and love from this Jesus. You must believe that if He is the Son of God, He will in some way answer your prayers.

I know that you feel for this Knight as I once did for mine, but you must also know that you have been placed on a painful path. Your love for your people is what you must follow. Here... I give you this as I gave Robert Goldheart the only other half. If ever you shall need him, he will always be there as your Protector Knight, know this all your days. As long as his heart beats, it beats for you and always will."

Chastity erupts in tears as she looks at what Agnes handed her. She also knows she will do what she must do for her people ..., but her heart will always belong to the Knight called Robert Goldheart.

The band of twelve, summon the gate keeper to open the castle gate. Horses and riders dressed for battle ride out into the brightly moonlit night. They all notice that they have never witnessed such brilliance from the heavens above in all their days. The twelve riders head up the hill, where their leader stops, and motions the men to continue. Turning around upon his glowing white steed, which seems to be absorbing the moons rays, he looks toward the tower, "I love you Lady Chastity of the Norse ... I truly, truly love you."

Turning Pegasus, the Knight hits the highpoint of the hill and disappears **over the horizon**.

A pair of swollen eyes high above had been watching, "I love you so much Robert Goldheart. May God protect you with his love throughout all your days, as I will always pray it so."
The weeping young Lady bears her sorrows, while in a window below her, someone else has also been watching and listening, and speaks quietly, "My love, please forgive me for I have bestowed the greatest pain upon our loving daughter, one I alone should have to bear."

PART 4

Much further west, in a higher tower and even bigger castle, two men sit drinking the finest of wines.

"You said that the Old Norse leader would accept my terms. You said Robert would perish against overwhelming odds. You said the Norse would decimate the entire Kings' Knights. You said I would negotiate a peace with the Norse from across the sea and be King over all. Yet here we sit. And now, I have to get married again to the Norse Lady. That part doesn't bother me as much. IF she is as beautiful, young, and pure as my brother has told you ... I shall truly enjoy the wedding night, before returning to my wicked ladies of the court. When does Víðarr launch his real forces? He has been paid mountains of silver. He will not get his hill of gold, until I am proclaimed, King."

The Bishop responds, "Edward how was I to know your brother Robert would gather the entire King's Knights against Víðarr?"

"I had no idea until today that Robert had this much influence and most of all, the King's trust. I know the plan was to get Týrs castle and use the excuse of Víðarr's marriage arrangement, but you and I know, that Norse son of Satan wants the whole of Europe including all those offspring of the female hounds in France. The Lady Chastity of the Norse will be on her way and here within three days. Call her a little bonus token of our agreement. Your agreement was that I soon become Cardinal, and possibly one day ... Pope. I will do all in my power to make you King, payoff the Norse to conquer across the waters, and even marry you to the virgin. I am sure you will become a widower for the third time soon. So, let us drink one more helping of this prestigious church wine, and then we retire with the ladies of the King's court."

Edward finishes his drink and retires into the arms of a few ladies. The Bishop of London awaits only one, the queen's Lady in Waiting, who tells the Bishop the secrets of the King and queen.

It seems the King shares all his rulings and future plans for his Kingdom with his wife. She in turn, cannot help but tell many things to her Lady in Waiting, not knowing of the harmful consequences toward her and her husband, the King.

PART 5

Robert, Henry, and the other ten rode until their steeds could ride no more. Stopping in a wooded area, there was a cool highlands lake with crystal blue waters before them. While the horses were treated to the refreshing waters, a few of the Knights broke out some refreshing spirits suitable for them. Others made camp to stay the night at this lake with its enchanted view.

Henry and Robert both being masters of the bow, decided to see if they could harvest a few pounds of venison to feed what will surely be a band of ravenous Knights.

Stalking slowly, the two hear some commotion within the forest. Both Knights know it is the sound of pursuit ... perhaps a stag with famished wolves at its hooves. Both men ready their arrows and pull back on their bows, waiting for the prey of the forest to come forth through a clearing.

Suddenly a figure bursts into the open; both men aim, and then abruptly lower their bows. Running at full speed, is a young boy. It did not take long before a group of four pursuers appeared, with one of them yelling,
"Stop you little heathen or I will drop you with an arrow! Living or not, we get paid the same!"

As the man drew his bow, so did the two men hidden in the brush.

Before the bowman can release his deadly arrow, two other arrows penetrate the man's forearm, forcing his tool of death to be dropped to the ground.

The boy glances back when he hears his pursuer wincing in pain. Still moving at a fast pace, the young eyes turn forward, and run straight into the massive arms of a huge bald headed man.

"Let me go! Let me go!" There is nothing the boy can do as Henry grabs the back of his britches and holds the struggling boy in midair.

The man with two arrows through his arm has his companions snap the shafts as he pulls the protruding tips out.

Another man steps forward, "Give the boy to us, he belongs to a noble. He is a runaway serf. I shall give you each a piece of silver for your troubles."

Robert looks at the suspended boy, who looks at him and quickly replies, "These jackals lie, I am no serf, and they are after many pieces of silver!"

Robert steps forward and looks into the eyes of the four men, one with clear pain in his eyes, the others ... eyes of lies.

Rubbing the stubble upon his face, Robert speaks, "It seems to me there is a truth in question. And being a man that has had many dealings with those who wish to fabricate stories, my friend and I will settle things, and take this boy with us to the nearest Lords castle to get clarity on this situation."

One of the four draws his sword and points it at the holders of their prize, "I warn you two, we are men who get paid very well to retrieve or kill. I now offer you ten pieces of silver each for that boy, and you two can leave with your lives."

Henry looks at Robert with the same look as if he just got surprisingly slapped by a maiden, "Robert, oh Robert, what shall we do? These four men have threatened us; I tremble so in fear that I may have to find a log to squat over!"

Robert trying to keep his composure, takes another step forward, "My friends, Henry the Bald and I, Robert Goldheart, shall hold on to this boy for now. But if you wish to die trying to take him, then it shall be so."

Now the four bad men are looking at each other in panic, as the man with two holes in his arm speaks, "You are them? I ... but we, must ... we have no choice as either way, we are doomed men."

One man draws his bow, but the Knight is quicker, and his arrow penetrates the man's heart. Another man charges with a sword in hand, while a massive hand draws his massive sword with one hand and hurls it at the oncoming target, cutting him almost in two.

The third man with a sword is upon Robert, and then stumbles past him, with a fatal wound to the throat. The last man, with the two holes still bleeding looks at his dead companions then at the two who slayed them, "I cannot go forward, nor can I retreat without which I was paid to retrieve. So goes the life of another man who has been paid in pieces of silver."

Drawing a dagger, the man plunges into his own heart and drops dead.

Henry and Robert look at each other, then at the boy, still being held above the ground, but no longer struggling. Robert looks into the young face and can see fear upon it,

"Boy you see, we mean you no harm and we can even possibly return you to wherever you have come from. But first, what is your name?"

Looking up as a long arm gently sets him down, the young lad proudly speaks. "I am Bain, son of Ronan, from the Isle of Ireland. It would be a long journey for you to return me to my homeland from which I was taken. But you can release me now. I know my way northward and have the skills to survive my way, if I'm given a sword."

The two men again look at each other with a smirk. Henry winks, "Lad, you may have my sword if you wish to retrieve it from that body there."

Bain agrees and walks over to the man with the blade buried within most of his chest. With all his might, Bain turns and twists and finally pulls the blade from the departed. Trying to lift it, he can just drag it along with him toward Henry. "Sir, I thank you for this sword, but I move quicker with a smaller one. I give this one back to you in exchange."

The two knights again try to hold back their laughter, as the proud looking lad stands before them. Robert reaches to his side and pulls out a more size appropriate weapon for the young brave hands, "Here ... this one shall do then."

The three are just about to move out when a crack of pine is heard. Suddenly a large stag appears, and is quickly taken with two arrows through its massive heart. Soon, a boy is dragging a sword, a Knight is carrying two bows, and a massive man is carrying a huge beast for a feast.

Back at camp with a fire going, and enough venison to fill all twelve and a half stomachs, the appearance of the stars and a moon close in on the group. Soon the forest rumbles from the sleeping sounds of full bellies.

A young voice quietly says, "Thank you Knights of Honor, someday I will repay." As the boy slips out into the darkness, one knight watches and knows this young man will make his way, **over the horizon** and back home.

PART 6

The band of twelve Knights rise at first light and head north, toward the castle of a nobleman, … the one who wishes to hire them to rid his lands of the Gaelic rebels from the north. As they ride into a valley, a sudden blast of horns begins to echo from all sides. Robert motions for the group to stop. They are all in the open with hills all around. Observing their surroundings, all eyes become alarmed as they watch the hillsides fill with hordes of men, to the left, and to the right … before them and also behind them.

Henry looks at Robert, "Well, it looks like we found what we're getting paid for."

Robert's eyes scour the surroundings, "My friend, I think I have led us into a predicament. Looks like a thousand wishing to do us harm."

Henry scowls, "Maybe closer to two thousand. We cannot charge uphill to the right or to the left, and from what I see in front, that option is also closed."

Looking forward they see long sharpened wooden shafts readied for a charge that would truly end the lives of their steeds. All eyes watch, and all ears hear the chanting and beating of swords upon shields. Robert looks into all the Knight's eyes that are with him ... not a single one has a flicker of fear within them.
There was only one thing to do.

Robert gave the order for the twelve to back their steeds into a circle, so when the masses descend upon the twelve, they can all charge out in twelve different directions and take as many to their graves as they can.

A sudden blow of a horn and the valley is filled with an eerie silence.

Roberts mind wanders back into the loving arms of what he so loves in this world. The few moments of passion, the tender touches, the laughter and the sorrow. Lady Chastity's likeness came into his mind, and it felt within his body and soul that she and he were still upon the terrace filled with the love of a lifetime.

Looking skyward, Robert closes his eyes, "Lord, I thank you ... for you gave me the love in just one day that so many can never find in a lifetime. Watch over my Lady Chastity, and guide us together once again when we get to your house ... Amen."

Opening his eyes, Robert, Henry and all the Knights know, this will be their last glorious charge. But it will be a death where all are honored, and all welcome.

The horns blast again, and the hordes charge forward ... coming from all directions.

Robert raises his sword, "Wait until they are within one hundred paces, then charge forward with all your might and send as many of them to the next world as you can. God have mercy on all our souls."

Robert can see a determined look on Henry's face. Taking off the massive helmet and dropping it to the ground, the bald head reflects the sun's rays.

The massive man looks over at Robert and smiles, "This should blind a few of these heathens long enough to take more than my share. It is a glorious day to die!"

With the twelve horses and twelve riders getting impatient for the finale, twenty four hearts pound for a last moment of glory.

Robert is ready to give Pegasus a last kick, "Fare thee well my friend, may you be spared to run free."

As Robert readies to drop his sword for the final time, a figure suddenly runs between the two foes waving and yelling. Within seconds, the charging horde has stopped and a dead silence is again upon this Valley of Death. A man rushes over to the figure and embraces it, and the figure returns the embrace. Distant words are spoken, and then two thousand combatants are given a signal to stand fast. Two figures walk toward the circle of Knights, and all eyes can see the boy who had feasted with them the night before approaching with a smile.

Coming closer, a tall man with long locks of red hair looks at Henry, "You must be this Henry the Bald, and next to you, Robert Goldheart. I am Ronan, leader of the Gaelic tribes. My son Bain has informed me that you rescued him from those who would harm him. You are not who I have come to destroy, but those I wish to give my thanks. There will be no harm to you on this day; you may ride off in peace."

Bain walks forward, "Looks like I have repaid a debt that I owed you Robert Goldheart and Henry the Bald, along with your men." Reaching to his side, the boys pulls out the smaller sword, "Here I return this to you as I have more than enough swords to return home."

Robert smiles at the young face, "Bain, it is yours, keep it and know it reflects our friendship."

The boy bows slightly, "I thank you Knight and honor your friendship." Smiling at the Knight he is given a smile and a wink in return.

Ronan walks forward and extends his hand, "I am still in your debt for giving me back what I feared was lost. I wait for the day to repay you. One last thing, beware of those you may trust. For I have learned of many deceptive things here in England. May the blessed One from the Holy Land watch over you."

With the shake of hands the two groups head in separate ways, but not before a final wave goodbye from a smiling young grateful face.

PART 7

Chastity sits quietly in a covered carriage as it enters the city of London. Sitting next to her, Agnes of Old can tell the young maiden has not yet left that special place in her heart and knows she will always be there. Týr and a few armed escorts ride along on horseback as the rest of the former Norse clan remained at the castle. Arriving at a checkpoint to the inner city, a guide sent by Edward is waiting. Motioning the group to follow him, he leads them to the Goldheart estate just outside the city.

The carriage and escorts make their way down a long entrance road, finally stopping at the front entrance. Looking down from a balcony four stories above, Edward and the Bishop stand watching.

Slowly the entourage prepares to enter the exquisite dwelling. First Agnes gets out of the covered carriage, then a young exquisite figure slowly appears, and both sets of watching eyes are immediately transfixed with lust.

The Bishops lips part, "You know Edward, I may need to Baptize her before you two wed."

Edward, who is still looking down at the Norse beauty, answers quickly, "Not this time, my overly passionate Holy Man. I think this one I will baptize myself ... for a while at least. And then I may give you the chance to taste the sweet nectar of this delicate Norse flower."

Agnes looks up and can see the two vultures upon their perch. She looks at Týr, "I have served you, and I have served your wife Astrid. I have been with Chastity since the time of her birth. But the moment you enslave your daughter to this bastard wolf, you will have to kill me, before I kill him and his bitch which stands beside him."

Týr is a taken aback by the words of the woman he has known for so many years, but has never spoken this many words at one time. Now more than ever before, the shame upon this father's face is also felt deep within his soul. Týr also knows that with this arrival, he may not leave without the nobleman's permission. The art of deception must be put into place, one thing Agnes of Old has always been master of.

Chastity holds her head high and walks gracefully into the entrance of the majestic estate. Her long blonde locks and her sparkling eyes, arouses many a guards fantasies with her exquisite beauty.

With her father leading the way, and Agnes at her side, Chastity looks up a winding stone staircase to see a porky Bishop followed by a thin man dressed in the most elaborate garments descending toward them, … "an English Peacock" Chastity thinks.

Bowing politely, two of the guests honor the host and Holy Man, but one stands firm with her old stone face ablaze.

Edward quickly walks toward them; his mind full of wedding night thoughts. The nobleman looks this young bride to be up and down, making the Norse princess's skin crawl. Extending his hand, Chastity does the same, only to have Edward grab it and kiss it like a dog licks a bone.

"Welcome to my home, my servants are yours, my food and drink are yours, my bedrooms are yours, until tomorrow night Lady Chastity of the Norse, then you shall share mine and be known as, Lady Chastity, wife of Edward Goldheart, maker and keeper of the King's riches."

Without warning, Agnes speaks up, "It is almost twenty-four hours until the wedding, the man and woman must not see each other within a day's time, for it brings the worst of luck. I will take Lady Chastity to her room now, unless you wish luck to be bad."

Edward looks at Agnes, "Old woman, you were not given permission to speak, I will forgive you this time, but from this time forward, you will ask to speak in my presence. Do you understand? This is not a request."

Agnes blinks twice, then glares at Edward and the Bishop, "Let me make myself clear, I have sworn my life to protect and will always do what is best for Lady Chastity! I will speak my mind and do what is best for the one I am entrusted. You can bare your weapons now and slay me, or forever hold your tongue toward what I have pledged"

Looking at the old woman, both Edward and the Bishop show a hint of fear from the old woman's words and facial expressions. Edward claps his hand and ten servants appear, "Show our guests to their quarters, and see to any comforts they may require. Lord Týr, my soon to be father, I bid you a nice day as I have things to look after, before my day to wed the Lady Chastity. Tonight, the men will dine and drink as a ritual."

Walking over and taking Chastity's hand and kissing it again with his saliva wet lips, "Until we meet in Holy matrimony tomorrow."
Looking into her eyes, Edward gives a lustful wink, as Chastity's stomach wishes to spew out what it contains.

The Bishop also excuses himself as he says, "I have a lamb in my flock to attend to."   Then both of these disgusting vultures fly out and are soon feasting upon their lustful prey of this day, the day before the wedding ...

Escorted to the third floor, Týr has his four personal escorts stationed outside of the room reserved for Chastity and Agnes. He also their room enters and shuts the door.

Chastity immediately looks at her father, "My wedding to this serpent is not the King's request, but it's a way for our people to have protection if needed against Víðarr and those who follow him. But father, I cannot marry this thin, beady eyed, salivating disgusting beast! He is vile!"

Týr, motions Chastity to calm down, and tone down her voice, as there may be eyes and ears upon them from within the walls. He looks at his loving daughter with the upmost concern,

"My dearest, please forgive me ... for this time I have placed the burden that we all should bear upon only you. And seeing this man, I also know, this wedding can never be. There is only one thing to do, and it must be so. The only way I can rid you of this parasite, and free you from this contract that I bestowed upon you ... tonight, as the men feast, I will drink with this Edward... we will toast together, and we shall both drink an Old Norse potion which will cause us both to sleep forever."

Chastity's eyes get big, "No father! You must not! I ... I ..."

Týr interrupts, "My dear child, it would be the only way no suspicion ever comes back to the Norse ... and ..."

Agnes sets a chair down hard, sits down, then looks up at the two, "Both of you, shut your tongues, and open your ears to an old woman's words."

As both father and daughter listen to the words and wisdom of the old woman, a new look comes over their faces, as her plan is brilliant! They are both thankful and relieved for another outcome. Now the game of deception must be played, without any mistakes, or Edward will win more than just what he now so wishes to have.

PART 8

The band of twelve Knights decided to pay the nobleman, who wished to hire them, a visit. Figuring that he doesn't know about the Gaelic's already heading back to their homes in the north, they can still see if this Lord can dish out a bit of silver, for which they surely would have died for, if not for saving a young boy named Bain.

As they near the Lord's castle, the Knights are about to descend down a hill when they spot two different groups of riders approaching each other. One clearly with the King's markings, the others were Víðarr's Norseman. Robert halts the group and motions them to be silent. All eyes from above watch as the two groups gather closer, not in a hostile manner, but one more of what appears to be friendship.

Although the words that are being spoken cannot be heard, their demeanor indicates that they are not combatants. Watching, they see that a small wooden chest is given to the band of Norsemen. The chest is briefly opened, and the shine within signifies that it can only be a chest of wealth. A few more words are spoken, and an Englishman points toward the direction that the twelve Knights had just come from. After a few more words are exchanged, the two groups head off in different directions.

Henry looks at Robert, "Now what do you suppose that was all about? Why would English soldiers be giving those arch enemies of the King of England, riches?"

Roberts's eyes glare straight ahead watching the two former foes depart, "Henry, I have a theory, but I know not yet the truth. That, my friend, we shall find out very soon."

Following the same path that the Englishmen had ridden, the now curious Knights know that this exchange is something that the Crown, which they have sworn to protect, knows nothing of.

As they ride, they see an exquisite castle before them; and they all know that the answers lay within its massive stone defensive walls. Now the game of cat and mouse must be played, so the twelve can find out in which direction the mice will scatter.

As they approach, the guard at the main gate waves them through, as they are expected.

Once within the walls, the entrance is closed, and the twelve follow a soldier to the stables. He points, "There Noble Knights, twelve reserved just for your coming. I will notify Lord Bernard of your arrival, he's been expecting you."

Robert bows his head in acknowledgement and the twelve dismount.

Putting their horses into private stables, Robert can see six other horses with perspiration upon them, knowing they have just come from a place where they were stealthily observed.

The twelve are received in the main hall by Lord Bernard and his wife, the Lady Anne. Bernard already has drinks waiting in silver chalices, "Come brave Knights, I have drinks ... the finest wine from Italy. I am Lord Bernard, cousin of the Bishop of London and cousin by marriage of Lady Anne, to the King. I welcome you, let us drink and feast ... and then we shall talk business."

Robert walks forward, and the Lady's eyes watch as they have not for many a year. "I am Robert Goldheart, leader of this group of Knights, sworn to protect the King, and England. We are appreciative of your hospitality, Lord Bernard and Lady Anne. Yes, we can certainly use food and drink, and then talk of what business needs to be had."

Looking over at the Lord of the castle, Robert notices, the Lady of the castle is staring, and communicating without words.

Within an hour of the first drink, eleven Knights have lady escorts at their sides for the feast. The banquet included smoked meats of wild boar, stag, and domestic swine, followed by roasted water fowl, pheasant, and chicken.

Robert sits and wonders, "Why has the Lord of this manor provided such an elaborate feast for him and his men? It is as if they are being served what their host thinks is, their last supper."

Robert also wonders why no maiden was provided to share a meal with him. He knows that a dinner companion would have been all that it would ever be, for he will always have in his heart, what his heart may never have.

Standing up from the table where his Knights are enjoying the festivities, Robert walks outside onto the walkway of the high walls.

He never expected that all of his movements were being watched by another.

The lonely Knight looks toward the moon as it is rising. He looks toward the southwest where London sits, in a manner that only the lonely can understand. His mind cannot envision what he held so close and what is so emblazoned within his heart, is soon to be within the chambers of his older brother.

Glaring **over the horizon**, a soft voice slows the breakage of his heart, "She is that special to you isn't she?"

Surprised, Robert sees the Lady Anne at his side. Noticing too, she is a Lady of extreme beauty, perhaps a few years his senior. "Lady Anne, you startled me, which to a Knight at times is difficult to do."

The Lady smiles, "Yes, but you never answered the question."

Robert looks into the eyes which he can see, have experienced much, "Yes my Lady... she is that special. There shall never be another like her in this world or the next."

Again the Lady smiles, "And yet, you looked at me as you look at who you love ... why?"

Robert knows the words are true, but digs deep down within his soul for the answer that quickly comes. "My Lady, I feel you too at one time had something so special in your life, but had to give up your greatest love, for what was best for the others you care for."

The Lady's expressions change, as her heart too remembers one so dear to it.

"Yes Robert Goldheart, Knight of my cousin the King, it was I who persuaded my husband, Lord Bernard, to not have a maiden at your side tonight, and as I told him it was better to talk business with an un-lustful man."

"When you first looked at me, I saw the same look I received from a Teutonic Knight long ago that I will always remember. You resemble him so much, that if I was not a Lady in love with the memories of so long ago, and you were not a Knight so deeply in love now, we both could easily fall in love. I know you know this, as I feel it."

Robert is stunned, as Lady Anne's words are true, for she is, perhaps what Lady Chastity will also someday be.

Lady Anne and the Knight stand and watch the stars appear ... both feeling a pain that they share. Robert looks over as the moon highlighting Anne's beauty, "What was his name, this Teutonic Knight?"

A smile returns as the Lady's heart remembers, "Johann Franz Zieboltz of Bavaria. I called him Hans. He was so handsome with his long locks of gold. He had those eyes ... much like yours ... that when you looked into them, no words were needed to know what was said."

"I know all about you, Robert. My husband has told me things that he had heard from his cousin the Bishop ... things that I know should never be told. Lady Chastity of the Norse, who is dearest to you, is in danger. I know that after your mother's death, your father gave little attention to you, and all his affection toward Edward. I also know he shunned you in his will upon his death. I know of Henry the Bald, who your mother entrusted with your care. But what you may not know, and what I must reveal to you Robert, your mother did share one night of passion with another. Her love of loves was a man called, Henry the Bald."

Now Robert is hit with a force no jousting match could ever bring. Lady Anne has just revealed that Henry the Bald may be ... his father.

Immediately Robert's memories of the big man flash before him. Henry had always been there for him, and taken him away from a loveless father at a young age.

Why Edward was always praised, while he would get his father's boot, now makes total sense. But Henry never talked badly of his father, nor ever challenged him. Something that oddly stands out of place for the Henry the Bald Robert has grown to know. After a minute of reliving his youth, Robert looks at Lady Anne, "He doesn't know does he?"

The Lady shakes her head from side to side, "No, not a clue. For as a young girl of twelve, I was sworn to secrecy."

Robert's confused eyes look into the Lady's eyes of truth, "So why do you bestow this on me now … something you had hidden inside for so long?"

Anne places her hand upon Robert's heart, "So you know the truth."

"You must not let your Lady of the Norse live with the same pain that your mother and I have felt."

"All the riches in all the Kingdoms of the world cannot buy a love so true. I shall help save two hearts that should be as one. I must now go before I am missed. I shall come to your quarters when the wine and ale have consumed my husband for this night."

Lady Anne quickly walks away and back inside, leaving a Knight's mind more scrambled than if hit with a battle axe.

"All the riches in all the kingdoms of the world cannot buy a love so true. I shall help save two hearts that should be as one. I must now go before I am missed. I shall come to your quarters when the wine and ale have consumed my husband for the night."

Lady Anne quietly walks away, she has more, leaving a knight's mind more astonished than if by a cannon ball...

PART 9

Týr is summoned to attend the pre-wedding festivities. Walking up to a son in law that will never be, "I have a request Edward, Agnes of Old must prepare a certain ring of twigs, herbs, and scents to be placed upon a brides head".

"It is a symbol of good luck and child bearing blessings on her wedding day. She will need to ride into the forests for her search. It is an Old Norse tradition still kept from the past religion. I will send one of my personal guards with her for her protection. But I need a pass so she and her protector can pass freely within your lands."

Edward raises his eyebrows, "This Agnes needs protection from what? For it is I, Týr, that thank *you*, for sending a guard along, to protect all those within my land … from her!"

Both start to laugh as Edward gladly gives Týr a pass. It was the, "child bearing" words that stirred Edwards's thoughts within, and did not give anything else another thought.

The two enter the grand room filled with the finest of foods and spirited drinks. There is also a wide range of maidens to accommodate and keep company with the male guests of the night.

The more Týr sees, the more he knows the right thing has been done. Tapping Edward on his shoulder, "Oh one last thing my soon to be son, could you have a servant prepare a drink of warm milk, honey, cinnamon and star anise and taken up to Lady Chastity's room at the end of our first meal? It too is a Norse tradition. One that brings forth more fertility and passion for a bride on her night of wed."

Now Týr has truly captured the would-be groom's attention. Summoning over his master of food and drink, the man is given strict instructions.

This drink must be made and sent up to Lady Chastity's chambers at the appropriate time.

Excusing himself briefly, Týr goes up to the quarters of Chastity and Agnes, assuring both that the pass and the drink for the bride to be will later arrive. Giving his daughter a kiss for luck, Agnes rushes him out as the long blond locks of a bride never to be, blows slightly from the warm winds of the night that rush through the room's openings.

With Týr headed back down to the festivities, Agnes looks at the guard at the door, "Be ready for I shall call upon you soon ... all is being prepared."

It did not take long for the alcoholic drinks to encourage loud sounds of talk and laughter. Týr, sitting in between Edward and the Bishop of London, can tell that many a maiden knows both of these men very well. The Norseman also knows he has made the best decision of his life, and prays that his daughter will again find what she so loves and desires by the next rise of a full moon.

Glancing out into the rooms hallway, Agnes and a guard appear, Týr nudges Edward, "Are you sure we should not ask Agnes of Old to join us after her nights findings?"

Edward and the Bishop's eyes both get big as the drink has touched their minds, "Týr, my soon to be father, that old woman would drive the devil out of hell." All three start to laugh as a Norse knows, the abundant consumption of wine and ale, brings the biggest fools to laughter.

Outside in the stable, Agnes shows the stable master the pass for herself and the guard. As the guard hops up on a steed, the stable master comes over to give Agnes a hand. About to give her a tush push, the old face turns, "Touch my behind and I shall remove both your hands and throw them into the swine's pen!" As he backs off, the Old Norse woman climbs up and the two riders are off to the gate, where again, their pass is shown and they ride into the night in search of what the old woman seeks.

Having finished his meal and a large quantity of drink, Edward summons the master of food over and barks out, "Have you readied the requested drink and all its ingredients for my wife to be?"

The man bows, "Yes my Lord, I am just about to take it up to your Lady's chambers myself."

Edward smiles "Let her know I'm ready for what this Norse drink is to bring tomorrow night."

Taking a big swig of wine, Edward makes eye contact with a certain maiden; both know that as soon as the father in law to be retires for the night, their night of lust will begin.

The master of food scurries away to carry out his duty. As he walks up the stairs past a house guard, to the future bride's door, he tells the personal guard, "This drink is for the Lady, and I must deliver it myself, with a message from her husband to be."

The guard momentarily pauses, then knocks on the door twice and announces, "My Lady, a drink with a message from Lord Edward."

The door is opened and the waiter sees a figure in a white dress facing out the window upon her knees. The long locks again slightly blowing in the wind. As he approaches, he hears in a whisper, "I am in prayer, please set the drink at the table."

The man does as told and then also whispers, "Lord Edward readies for what this drink will bring for tomorrow night."

Slightly bowing, and without turning around, the words, "Thank you" are whispered.

The master of food leaves, and the door is shut by the guard who stands there in watch. Making his way past the house guard again at the stairs, he heads back down and to his Lord's Table; the delivery of the drink and the message given to the Lady is confirmed.

Týr now finishes his chalice of wine with a smile, as he can see; it is time for him to retire. Looking at Edward, "My soon to be son, I bid you goodnight as I am not as young as I once was. I do have a bride to present to you tomorrow and I need rest. Sleep well, for I know, I shall." With the happiest of looks upon his face, Týr stands and walks toward the staircase then gallops up them to his sleeping quarters with biggest of smiles.

No sooner had he left, than a well-endowed maiden was upon the Lord of the estates lap, with more than just drink on her mind.

Part 10

With the nights darkness starting to give way to light gray, the once lap sitting maiden makes her way out of the master chambers. Within a few seconds, a loud voice is heard throughout the large stone hallways, "What do you mean they never returned? This is unacceptable!"

Edwards's foggy head and exhausted body gets slowly up and slips on a robe, walking toward the commotion. Seeing Týr talking to one of the guards at the top of the third floor staircase, one of Týrs guards is also being given a talking to.

Edward approaches more groggy than alert, "Can a man who is to be married this day at least sleep until the rise of the sun?"

Týr walks over to Edward, "Agnes of Old and the guard I sent with her have not yet returned!"

"The gathering of what was needed by this old woman, has never taken this long in all the years of Norse marriages. I suspect foul play of the worst kind."

Rubbing his eyes, Edwards's thoughts begin to flow through the aftermath of the night before drinks, "I am sure there is some explanation, I will check with the gate guard and stable master."

Týr looks at the pathetic man who wishes to wed his daughter, "I have already done that! We must let Lady Chastity know, for if foul play is involved, this wedding cannot be on this day." Walking toward his daughter's room, and looking back at Edward, "You must stay there, for a groom is forbidden to see his bride before the wedding."

Knocking on the door, there is no answer. Knocking again, Týr just enters to see nothing. Even the bed has not been slept in. The windows' still open, a cool morning breeze blowing through. Yelling for Edward and his guard, all eyes can see, Lady Chastity is nowhere to be found.

Týr points his finger at Edward who is clearly confused, "I blame you if my daughter was taken by evil ones! And if this is some kind of trickery on your part, I will not stand for it!"

Edward is totally lost for words as he stumbles about the chamber in confusion. Ordering his guard to wake the master of food and drink and bring him forth, it is as if the Lady just disappeared. A few moments later, the last man to see Chastity the night before is telling all that she was there, her white dress, long blond hair slightly blowing in the wind, on her knees praying out the opened window. She had even talked to him and thanked him for her drink, then went back to her prayers.

Týrs face is red as he looks at his guards, "Ready our horses, we ride for an audience with the King."

Now Edward is in a state of panic as Týr and three of his remaining men prepare to go to the King for answers.

The four Norse ride out the gate before Edward can gather his thoughts, dress and also prepare to ride to the King. Týr and his men reach a crossroad. As they stop, Týr looks at his men with a smile as a young rider approaches from behind, "Well done. We take our losses and ride back to our castle. We must prepare for another onslaught from Víðarr soon, but now with no support. Agnes of Old truly is the wisest of the wise and master of all trickery. Well done men, now come, my daughter and Agnes await us."

Riding across a river, the young rider opens a leather bag and dumps the contents into the moving waters, "I shall never do that again!"

All start to laugh, as a white dress and headdress wreath with the remnants of long golden locks weaved into it flow gently away with the waves. Týr smiles at the young guard who had portrayed Lady Chastity. So it seems an old woman's wisdom outwitted a powerful nobleman.

A Lady had been transformed into an apparent guard, while a guard had been transformed into an apparent praying, blonde haired whispering lady in white.

After this royal embarrassment, Edward had cleared his mind of the previous night's drink and folly, and realized there would be no wedding to Lady Chastity of the Norse. His anger within begins to boil. Eyes once filled with lust, are filled with images of the executioners blood soaked axe. "Rest assure you Norse that have played me, your time comes more quickly than you think."

PART II

It had been an eventful night in London. For as the dark early hours of a new day appeared, so did a Lady to a Knight's chamber. Lady Anne had come as she had promised, but it was not for passion in the night. Quickly letting Anne enter, and closing the door, Robert could see the Lady was in dire thought.

"My Lady Anne, I must say, I feel uncomfortable if any eyes were to know of your venture here in these early hours."

Looking at Robert's worried face, "You need not worry for I go for early morning strolls often. More so because my husband indulges too much in drink, then brings forth the howling sounds of a she bear giving birth with every breath. I will make this quick. Knight Robert Goldheart, who do you serve? Where is your heart pledged?"

Motioning the Lady to take a seat, Robert sits next to her, "My Lady as I have not much wealth, I serve those who are willing to pay for myself, Henry the Bald and our ten Knights. But rest assured, we are, and forever will be, pledged to serve the King and England, so help us God."

Anne smiles, "I was hoping those would be the words I hear Robert. I have come upon evil here that wishes to overthrow my cousin the King".

"There are a few rich and powerful noblemen involved in this plot. But as of now, I know of only three, the Bishop of London, your half brother, Edward Goldheart, and the rumbling bear in my quarters, Lord Bernard."

Robert is a bit surprised, but not shocked, as things that he had questioned, are now making sense. "Lady Anne you must bring this forth to the King right away, before it's too late."

Touching Robert's hand, "I cannot, as I have no written proof. Just what my ears have overheard from what was spoken on an early morning a month past, as I was strolling about. They wish to bring the Gaelic tribes down upon the northern lands for the killing of a tribal Lords son. They are also in a deadly alliance with Víðarr of the Norse, to whom they have paid many riches. Between both of these forces, they will surely weaken the King's Knights and men, and that is when they will strike at him, and that is when your brother takes the crown."

Roberts's ears have just heard what his heart has known for some time. It all makes sense, even the marriage of Lady Chastity. Standing up, he begins to pace, "You don't suppose that Týrs involved with this do you? And why can't you just go warn the King, he will believe your words, even if you have no written proof. At least when things come into play, he will know your words were true."

"But, you need not worry about a Gaelic leader's son; he is safe with his father, as on our way here we had, by the grace of God, rescued the boy, who later rescued twelve Knights from thousands. But we must not let the conspirators know of this, for it shall be perhaps the Achilles heel to their plans." Walking over and taking the Lady's hand, "My Lady, I pledge my service to you and the King. Tomorrow we shall take you on your way to him."

Lady Anne shakes her head, "I may not leave this place, for Bernard has suspected that I know of what may be coming forth. He has stated, if ever I was not to be found ... all servants which were bestowed on me long ago ... men, women, children and even the old, would be killed."

A distant rooster crows as two minds think, Robert looks into the eyes of the Lady, "You must go before the bear awakens. I will stay as long as possible as your husband still thinks the Gaelic horde is lurking about."

"I will find more answers, and proof for you and the King. One last question ... this Germanic Knight called, Franz Zieboltz of Bavaria, what became of him?"

The Lady thinks this an odd question, "Sir Robert, for many years I had paid informants to bring answers. Last known he went to the Holy Land and became a protector of those who would go on the pilgrimage there. But alas, there has been no news in many a year. Why you ask this?"

Robert gives Anne a kiss on the cheek, "A great Lady needs only one protector, and for now, I shall be the one."

Lady Anne leaves as quick as she came, while the Knight looks somberly out a window **over the horizon**, not knowing that the girl he loves with all of his heart is not yet married to his brother, the traitor.

PART 12

Týr was overjoyed to see the harsh blank face of Agnes the Old and the newly shorthaired version of the Lady of the Norse at their rendezvous point. It would be a very quick trip back to their small castle. Edward and the Bishop should have figured things out by now, and they know that they will be on their own when Víðarr brings his horde.

Now they must all prepare to defend their castle to the last man, woman and child, for all they all know that Víðarr will not give even the last newborn quarter.

PART 13

"That son of a female dog! He and his old witch and young flower ... may they rot underneath the large swollen feet of Víðarr and his stench ridden band of cutthroats! Embarrass me in front of the King and his court??? I will soon chop their smiles off their Norse heads!"

A chalice of wine is poured as the Bishop almost smiles, "Oh Edward you are so dramatic, come have a drink of wine as I need you not to boil over, we have many plans. I have sent twenty five percent of the church and nobility offerings to Rome. I have also put away twenty five percent for each of us. Given the last twenty five percent of the King's wealth, Víðarr will bring the largest group to ever invade these lands."

"Remember, we have allies on the southern coast, allies in the north, and your favorite Norse, Týr, will have to try to stop it all in the middle with his small clan. Within a moon and a half, you will be on your way to being … King!"

Edward grabs a chalice and pours a good helping of wine, drinking it down, he looks at the calm faced Bishop, "You know what I need right now?"

The Bishop takes a drink, "Yes, I do. That maiden whose bustle is overflowing more than any glass of wine you have ever poured!"

A smile appears on a man wishing to be King. "You know me well, my soon to be Pope."

PART 14

Convinced that the Gaelic band from the north
is a threat, Lord Bernard decides that he would
rather have Robert and his Knights die in battle,
rather than those loyal to him. And so it came to
pass that the twelve Knights rode out in search of
a battle. Already paid in silver, they know that
there is really no battle to be fought. Henry and a
few others have brought concealed bottles of
wine, and a few loaves of bread along. Finding a
stream with enough foliage for their steeds, the
twelve dismount and indulged in the peaceful
serenity. Dividing up the day's pay from Lord
Bernard, the morning and afternoon was
proclaimed for eating, drinking, and relaxation.

Robert found a tree with many branches and
leaves to lie under in the cool shadows, having had
his fill of wine and bread.

Briefly closing his eyes, the thoughts of a day, not long ago, fills his mind. With memories of Lady Chastity in his heart, a sudden, "SNAP!" from above brings the dreaming, heartbroken Knight back to the present. Looking up, Robert sees an old gray haired man high in the tree looking down.

Jumping up, "You there! What may you be doing? A spy perhaps, for Lord Bernard?"

The small older man knowing he has been found out, starts to climb down as others around also come over on full alert. Reaching the last of the taller branches, the man drops to the ground, surrounded by the twelve.

Smiling he speaks, "Well, I sure hope you have a bit of wine and bread left for a famished thirsty old man."

Robert looks at the short man, "What may be your purpose? From your talk, I'd say you are a Gaelic. Why are you watching us? And, what name are you called?"

Brushing himself off a bit from the bark and leaves, an old smile forms, "I am Mica. Ronan has put me on a task of overseeing your well-being. As he stated, there is evil among your Kingdom. And there are those who have an alliance with an evil that shall take not just these lands, but wants all the lands beneath your feet, as well as those beneath Ronan and us Gaelic. I am here to help us all, as Ronan makes ready for what is coming, something that you and your King do not know."

Robert looks at Henry and motions for him and Mica to follow him to where they can talk more of this and see what needs to be done before it is too late. It is soon learned that Mica knows more than the Knights on things going on in their Kingdom.

Giving the older gent a bottle and a loaf, Robert and Henry begin to hear so much of what Ronan wished to say. Then Mica speaks the words that bring both Knights to full alarm. It's the news of Edward, the Bishop, Bernard and others, involved in the conspiracy to overthrow the King.

Mica's information confirms that over twenty thousand of Víðarr's Norse, supported by warriors paid off by his brother Edward and the Bishop, will invade England like locusts on fields of wheat. The two Knights hear what so many among the isles of England wish to never hear.

But it is the last thing the old Gaelic man says that stands out, "The first to be wiped out by the Norse invaders will be those that fled with their new religion. These include their leader, an old wise woman, and a Lady of the Norse that never married."

Now Robert is overwhelmed. He wishes nothing more than to rush to the Lady's castle, and fulfill what is within their two hearts. But he cannot just yet, for he has pledged his support of a Lady he knows is in more danger than even she realizes.

PART 15

Týr had found some prized written works while at Edward's estate. Reading one in Latin, the old leader gets an idea for a defense of his castle and those living within. Knowing that Víðarr and his followers will make ladders to scale the walls in overwhelming numbers, he studies a story of the Roman coliseum and how certain special effects were used to dazzle the crowds. It was a tale of a ring of fire, and the details on how the Romans accomplished it. This intrigued Týr.

He must now put all those within his castle on a steady task of preparing for what he knows will soon come, yet knows not, that it will be sooner than expected.

While metal is forged, clay is formed and dried, and foliage is heaped around the castle walls.

All work hard, including the leader, an old woman, and a short haired Lady. They all do their part from sunrise to sunset.

It wasn't until the sun was kissing the day goodbye that the Lady finally rests on the terrace, thinking back to a time when she was within the arms of the Knight that her heart will always belong to. Knowing that he is out there with Henry the Bald and only ten others, she cannot help but fear something bad could happen, and what she so loves could be lost forever, before the two hearts can again beat as one.

Holding something dear in her hand, she walks over to an exhausted Agnes, "You once told me, that if I sent this, and it would reach him, he would come … no matter what. Agnes, can you make it so? I have no way of even knowing where he is. He may be off to other lands fighting, not knowing that I never became a bride. I miss him so very dearly."

The old woman sees the tears of sorrow and worry forming on the young girl before her. With a soft touch of her hand, "Give it to me; I will make sure that he gets it. I know of one who can make it through the groups of assassins waiting on the paths leading from here. It may take some time, but I know, he will come."

Giving a reassuring hug to Chastity, the old mind is thinking, "I pray it's not too late."

Having placed Lady Chastity's object into a small pouch, it is now placed over the head of the one chosen to find its recipient.

Looking into the eyes of the young courier, Agnes speaks, "Your father was a great man of the woods, and one who could survive within them. Remember what you have been taught; for now you must be the master of the woods. Go and find Robert Goldheart, for I have learned that he may be north of here, hired by a Lord. Trust no one but those you have been sent to find. Make your fallen father proud, Rolf."

The young eyes sparkle, and the boy of thirteen heads on his way in the dark of night. He is to ride all night, and then he and his horse must stay hidden during the day. The boy had been taught since a very young age to read the stars at night and the shadows of the day. It was also the hope of the old eyes that if this lad was spotted he would gather no interest to those lurking among the roads. Three messengers had already been sent to the King, but only one horse covered in blood stains had returned, confirming Edward is blocking all communications in or out.

Part 16

Robert and Henry have learned much from Mica, and the plot now comes into view. Víðarr knowing the north and south are aligned with Edward and the Bishop, just needs to wipe out his former Norseman in the middle. Once the panic of the invaders spreads throughout the land, Edward and the Bishop will take over, and relieve the King of his thrown. Robert and Henry also hear of other possible allies, just across the channel in the land of the Normans. When Robert learns of this, it is decided that two of his men will be sent to ask for their help. Time is now also their enemy, for there is little of it to be wasted. But first, Robert must keep his pledge to Lady Anne, before he can go to what he so desires. It is Henry that comes up with a possible way for Robert to keep his pledge and get back to Lady Chastity.

Looking at the massive bald man, Robert smiles, "Well, let's get this plan of yours started."

In a blink of an eye, the massive hand strikes Robert in the face, leaving his nose to be reset and some good bruising. Eight other Knights are also told to dirty themselves and show signs of battle with cuts and swellings. Then the plans are told. Mica and two clean Knights shall go toward the next valley and build as many campfires as possible. The rest will quickly ride back to Lord Bernard and tell him of thousands of Gaelic men who have gathered for battle and are preparing what they need to scale the walls of his castle. Robert will also mention that two of his Knights have fallen and they have found out that the son of the Gaelic leader was killed by men under his banner, and they are there to destroy all.

Riding back through the gates and beyond the walls of Lord Bernard, Robert can see the man has panic upon his face.

Lord Bernard sees that his hired Knights are now two less, and the remaining ten look like they've been in a serious battle. Robert asks Bernard to have his captain of the guard ride out with him and Henry that evening to observe the landscape.

Doing so, the man loyal to Bernard sees over a hundred fires burning within the valley. Knowing that each fire may have twenty five or more men, it appears as if a massive force is getting ready to scale the walls and kill all within. The now shaken captain brings the news back to his Lord, resulting in panic, which is soon replaced by fear in the eyes of the master of the castle.

Summoning his men, Bernard looks at his wife, "Quickly! Gather your things … there are thousands of the Gaelic's ready to strike, we must leave for the safety of the west tonight!"

Lady Anne looks at the cowardly man and speaks, "And what of the others? Those who serve you and I. My personal staff here within ... what's to become of them?"

Bernard barks his response, "Let them fend for themselves, run and hide, or stay and die ... it matters not to me. I shall come back and reclaim what is mine, once these barbarians slither back to their huts in their land."

Anne cannot believe that this is even a man before her. With a stern face, the Lady speaks loudly, "I shall not and will not abandon those who have served me well. You go and run with your men; we shall stay and fight to the last. I still have ten brave Knights who have pledged a vow. Go Bernard, and tell the King how you left his cousin to perish, while saving your worthless behind."

Bernard gathers up more of his wealth and looks over at his wife, "It matters no to me as soon, you will no longer be the cousin of any King."

Anne's eyes turn to rage as she has now been given the confirmation of her husband's betrayal, "You are lower than a swine beneath another swine's hooves. May you, and those who conspire with you, rot in the deepest depths of the hell you all deserve."

Raising his hand to strike his defiant wife, Bernard's hand is stopped in midflight by one who is sworn to protect the Lady. Looking at the coward before him, the Lady's protector firmly speaks, "You will NOT strike this woman! Hurry and flee, before it is more than those outside these castle walls you have to fear."

With a sheepish look, Bernard turns, gathers his wealth and is soon running down the staircase and to an awaiting horse. Taking his most loyal men with him, Bernard takes one last look back, "Fare thee well, once cousin of the King, and the Knight who you have seduced."

Lady Anne's look of anger is quickly replaced by one of great concern.

Looking at Robert she again speaks, "We must prepare to fight and to die. There are not many, but we shall fight."

Robert, impressed with the Lady's courage, gives her a sly smile, "My Lady, rest assured ... there will be no dying or fighting on this day or the next. But we must gather up all and move southward. What your cowardly former husband fears so much, is not really there. But I have learned there will soon be others who will come. All should fear them, as they come to kill and destroy." Robert continues, telling the Lady Anne how the leader of the Gaelic's has become more of a friend than foe, they must prepare to go help another Lady dear to his heart that will soon be in need of his protection.

With mornings first light, all are informed to gather what belongings they can. As Robert is helping Lady Anne gather a few things, he is suddenly interrupted by a young voice.

"Knight Robert Goldheart, I come with a message for you."

Turning around, Robert sees a young lad ready to hand him a pouch. Taking the item, Robert opens it to see something familiar. Looking at the young eyes, "You have traveled far lad; is Lady Chastity safe and well?"

The lad speaks quickly, "Yes she is for now. Agnes of Old had me bring this to you; she said you would know what it means."

Patting the boy on his head, "And what may this brave young man be called?"

The boy gives a confident look, "I am Rolf, son of Han, master of the woods. My father perished in the fight against Víðarr, but I will someday avenge my father's death."

Robert can tell the boy is as proud as he is brave and smart, "Rolf, we leave soon toward Týr and Lady Chastity. I would be honored if you ride with the Knights along the way."

The Knights' words have truly enriched a young proud heart beyond expectation. The lad shall ride between Robert and Henry the Bald, holding his head higher than any clouds above.

Having gathered up some belongings, food, and weapons of war; the band of mostly women, children, and old men, follow a Lady's carriage. The carriage is being led by the special Knights, and a young brave heart.

It will not take Lord Bernard long to figure out that he was tricked by those loyal to the King. Bernard also knows that the last words he spoke to his wife could have his head removed, if she were to get an audience with her cousin, the King. Due to this, he has hired two assassins ... just in case Víðarr does not arrive in time to silence his now estranged wife. Heading for the safety of Edward and the Bishop, he is pleased to hear, that their paid Norsemen have started their landings.

News has also come that those he left behind are on route to where the major onslaught of twenty thousand Norse will converge.

A small castle, unknown to the King, will have to defend his crown. Hearing this, Bernard now relaxes as he knows; his wife and her protector will soon be no more. The three evil conspirators are soon indulging in food, wine, and the willing maidens of their lust beside them.

Part 17

A rider approaches quickly and is waved through the open gate of a castle. He rushes quickly up to Lord Týrs chamber. All watch in fear, wondering what the news may be. They have not yet completed the defensives that have been put before them at the castle.

Rushing in as Týr is speaking with Lady Chastity, both sets of eyes become alarmed. "My Lord, a group is descending upon us from the north!"

"There are riders in the lead followed by a force of a few hundred baring supplies."

Týr is about to ask more questions when an old voice blares out, "These are not hostiles, but those who Rolf, son of Han, has found. They are led by Robert Goldheart and they come to fight with us."

No sooner had the words flowed from an old pair of lips, when Chastity's eyes light up as if filled with the energy of the sun. An old half smile and a wink to a now anxious Lady, brings a touch of joy to a relieved father's heart.

Rushing around trying to put on her finest for the Knight she so holds dear, a glance in the mirror brings a touch of sorrow to her. Running her fingers through her hair, she is still looking more like a lad then a lassie. Suddenly an old voice rings out, "Oh for the love of Thor, put it to rest, he cares not for what's on top, but what's within. Put on the dress that enhances your bosom. That attracts a man, like a beehive does a bear."

Smiling, the Lady is soon dressed and ready to welcome back into her life what she never thought would be possible.

Henry looks over at Robert as the two lead the group of displaced people through the entrance of the small castle, "What be it with you? You look as if you drank some bad goat's milk."

Robert's insides have never felt this way before as he waits to see what he so loves. "Henry, I have never felt like this before ... ever. I am as if I was within my first battle but ten times worse. Have you ever had that feeling?"

Henry chuckles a bit, "Knight, you are truly in love." Getting a somber look upon his face Henry softly speaks, "Yes Robert, there was one a long time ago, gave me that feeling. I will always hold her dear to my heart for all of my days." The words bring a smile to Robert's face as he now truly knows what Henry doesn't.

Stopping and dismounting, Robert goes to the carriage of Lady Anne. Helping her down, the mature attractive Lady places a kiss upon Robert's cheek, "Thank you for saving not only I, but all of those left behind by my swine of a husband."

Lady Anne smiles at her Knight, "Go! For whom you love awaits you! She is already cutting me to pieces with her eyes. It's a woman thing, be not alarmed."

Seeing the face that is no longer framed by the long locks of sunshine, the eyes meet and engulf two hearts that had never believed that they could be together again. No words were spoken, just an embrace that filled many on lookers with nearly the same joy as the two lovers. The father knows that his daughter is where she should be, and an old woman knows it must be, for days are short.

Týr welcomes Lady Anne and all of her people to his palace, where they are given a place to stay by those already within the walls. With the new help, Týr now knows that what he has planned for a defense will be completed within a few days. After telling Robert of his fortifications, the Knight is impressed with the plan. Having brought some needed items with them from the north, there are still things that must be readied for what all know will come soon. Besides the domestic forms of fat and meat, Robert sends out a few good men, and a new friend, the young woodsman ... in search of wild boar. All work as one for survival.

PART 18

As night falls, Týr has a table set for Robert and his Knights, as well as for Lady Anne, Agnes, and their new hero, Rolf.

But before the meal is to be served, Robert unsheathes his sword and gets on his knees before Týr. He places his trusted sword in both of his hands and holds it out hoping for a positive outcome. "Lord Týr, I cannot wait a moment longer. I present to you my sword in which I hold my honor. I humbly request permission to ask your daughter, the Lady Chastity, for her hand in marriage. I swear to you and before God, I will always love her and be faithful to her. I will protect and cherish your daughter for all my days, so help me God."

Týr can see that all at the table, especially the hopeful future bride, awaits an answer. Now comes the moment all have waited for. Putting his hand on Robert's lowered head, "Sir Robert Goldheart, Knight of the King, you have my blessing to wed my daughter. I know her heart belongs to you. But as Lord of this castle and with all the priests called back by the Bishop, a true Christian wedding cannot yet take place. We must deal with this evil before us first. I know that you will make me proud being the son I never had. I give you my permission, now it is up to what God has in store for there to be a blessed date."

All at the table know Týrs words are true as he has blessed this engagement. But they also know that it is truly in God's hands now. The mature attractive Lady Anne gives her own blessing in words for the two, as she feels at least one Knight's and a Lady's love can go forward.

Lady Chastity hearing the heart filled words by Lady Anne, now feels a bit ashamed for her earlier thoughts, as she now knows that this Lady once had a special love, but never had the chance to let it fill her heart.

Not known to those within the castle, this will be the last peaceful night. It will also be the last night that the two, who are so in love, can again embrace for a few moments, all while an older woman searches for a chamber pot.

PART 19

Having sent out one of his Knights while all slept, Robert needed to know what is happening to the east near the coast.

Týrs plan for the castles defense was almost complete as the surveying Knight came riding up quickly out of breath, "Robert! They have landed, thousands of them! They have near as many ships as we have men! In the valley they are building ladders to use to scale the walls. I saw terrible things! A prisoner was taken aboard a ship, tied to a rope and as it went out a short distance, the man was cut and thrown into the waters as the rowers slowly moved the vessel. Víðarr sat aboard, eating, while the man in the water let out horrifying screams. Sharks Robert; they sat and laughed and ate, while the man was torn apart by sharks, then they threw out another. They come within a day or two!"

Robert didn't even have time to respond when a voice high up on the wall spoke, "They'll be here tomorrow, could be day … or night … but they will be here tomorrow."

Looking up, they see an older man sitting carefully on a slim shelf of one of the castle towers. Robert calls up, "Mica, again you surprise me. I find it hard to believe you sit there; come on down, I hope you bring good news."

The old legs scale down the structure like a normal man climbs down a ladder. Reaching the bottom, Robert knows Mica must be again in need of a bite and drink. Walking along the way to Týrs kitchen, Mica lets Robert know that Ronan and his band are on their way and picking up every available man along the way. But, they may not make it to them for three or four days. This time frame means that it will take everything they have to survive and fight off what is coming. Giving Mica some bread and roasted fowl, his old eyes wander to see something that catches his eye.

"Who is she? I see her walking about. She is beautiful. What may she be called?"

Robert looks over and sees Chastity walking with her familiar old escort. Giving Mica a smile, "Oh I see you have found what I fight for and will die to protect. That is the Lady Chastity of the Norse, my wife to be."

Mica looks up at Robert, then over at the two women, then back again, "Isn't she old enough to be your mother?"

Robert now looks confused; "You are talking about the younger of the two are you not?"

Now Mica's eyes get big, "Now why would I think young skinny lass with hair like a lad would attract an older gent as myself? I talk of the fine mature maiden who escorts the boyish one."

Now Robert looks over, then back at Mica who he now thinks must have a vision problem.

Nonetheless, Robert takes Mica over for an introduction. Approaching the two, Chastity quickly runs into the arms of Robert.
"Mica of the Gaelic's, this is Lady Chastity of the Norse, my wife to be."

Mica gives the Lady a bow, "A pleasure Lady Chastity. Now who may this beautiful Lady be that walks with you?"

As Robert looks at Chastity and Chastity back at him, the old Lady is caught off guard, as it has been almost as many moons as stars in the sky since she was called beautiful. Robert clears his throat, "Mica, this is Agnes."

No sooner said then a leg kicks the Knight in the shin, "I am called Agnes of Old. Remember your manners, Robert Goldheart!"

While a Knight rubs his shin, and a young short haired Lady giggles, Mica gently takes Agnes's hand and places a tender kiss upon it. "It's a pleasure to meet you, Agnes of Old."

Chastity and Robert wait for some kind of retribution from the feisty one, instead she looks at the old Gaelic, "You must have come far, come let me show you where you can get some food and drink."

Ready to walk away with Mica, Agnes looks back at the two stunned onlookers, "Behave yourselves, or you shall feel my wrath!" Turning and walking with the older gent, it's as if Agnes's features turned from cold darkness to a warm light.

PART 20

Three silver chalices clink together and wine is consumed in a festive manner. The newest at the table smiles, "And so tomorrow it will begin. Víðarr will strike Týr and his group to destroy them all, including my soon to be dead wife! Hopefully they can accomplish this as quickly as the three of us can eat this glorious meal!" Edward again gets his familiar crocodile smile, "And the Lady Chastity, among the dead as well. I just hope Víðarr and his men have their brutal ways with all the women before they are disposed of."

The Bishop is a bit more cautious, "You two forget that Víðarr must survive this first battle, retaining as many men as possible, to show strength, and send fear within the population. The King is relying only on the Lords from the north and south to gather and strike!"

"If they don't, and Víðarr is within the Kings boundaries, then we can finally dispose of the King, and bring forth the new King!   Edward, Redeemer of the English."

All three again drink a toast as a Bishop stands, "I bid you goodnight as I have a personal little confession time waiting with the queen's Lady in Waiting."

Now all three men have sinister smiles as Edward summons a few maidens for his own, and Bernard's nightly entertainment.

PART 21

The candles have already burnt down as Týr, Robert, Henry, and the other remaining eight Knights talk of strategy. With all four walls secured by Týrs plan, and the driest foliage gathered close to the walls, they are all confident they can survive the first onslaught. It is the next few days afterward, that all know is uncertain.

Whether it be help from the Norman Knights coming from the south, or from Ronan in the north, they must do all they can to buy time. And with daylight approaching, all must get what rest they can, knowing that if things go wrong, they will all be resting in eternity.

PART 22

A massive, still warm heart is held in a hand, with the flicker of the campfire casting an eerie glow, a bite is quickly taken out of it, and then passed to the next hand. With each large bite, the heart of a once majestic stag is consumed by those around the fire with the red glow of its embers, as if they were at the entrance to hell. With a small piece of the once mighty heart returned to the one who took the first bite, Víðarr quickly chews it down. With the blood on his face illuminated by the flames, a sword is raised, and words are barked out, "Death to all the men, women, and their offspring!" Taking a big drink of mead, Víðarr smiles, "But I shall have my way with both Lady Chastity and then Lady Anne, before I turn them over to all of you!"

"Plunder and kill! Plunder and kill!" The words are spread throughout the massive groups gathered around their fires. The chant echoes loudly throughout the smoke and fire filled valley, making even the devil feel at home.

PART 23

Chastity sits silently looking outward **over the horizon** as the first signs of the day start to filter through the darkness. Soon she is joined by Lady Anne, and an almost dreamy Agnes of Old. No words are spoken out loud, but all are communicating with God above. They know that for many within these walls, it will be their last day on this earth. All three sit close and hold hands to give each other the strength they will need. They know the plan. All the men and women will be involved in this battle for life.

Whoever can pull back a bow will do so, sending a volley of arrows upon those outside the walls. Children old enough to carry arrows for the bow masters will help until all arrows are gone. Those too old or too young, will shelter in a place in the lower castle chamber.

If the walls are breached, women and children shall flee down a passageway that Týr had constructed. Once all are in this secret passageway, a wall will be collapsed to give some the chance to flee out of a hidden tunnel and into the woods. All men will fight to the death, for it will be quicker death than being tortured by Víðarr' as a prisoner. They must try to hold out for the Gaelic's of the north and the Normans from the south.

Meanwhile, Henry the Bald sits sharping his massive blade to a razors edge. Looking around, he sees eight other Knights doing the same, each within their own thoughts of the battle to come. It is just Robert who is standing high above in an observation tower watching the eastern skies.

With a touch of fog beginning to hug the land around the castle, a distant hillside seems to be in movement. The dead silence of the haze and mornings first light is abruptly broken by the massive sounds of, "**BOOM! BOOM! BOOM!**"

The sound gets louder and louder as it echoes from all sides of the castle.

Robert stares onto the gathering hillsides, "It will not work here Víðarr, this Mongol tactic of sending fear upon us. Bring forth your hordes of paid mercenaries, for many will never collect."

Within the walls, they have kept many fire ambers hot, Týrs brilliant plan of defense will soon be tested.

With the thunderous sounds penetrating the stone walls, some are in fear, others just curious, and those which are battle tested rest until called upon. Henry joins Robert up high to survey the situation.

Seeing the masses gather, Henry blurts out, "Like termites upon a mound they gather. I think that they shall not strike during the day, but will try a night attack, with a barrage of torches for display."

"I am not much of a praying man Robert, as I have killed many a man and only fear my judgment for that … but as this daylight broke and the thunder started, I did tell God, that I will send as many of these Norse as I can, His way. I am not scared to either live or die but I am scared for those I cannot protect."

Looking at the man who has no clue that he is talking to his son, Robert says "Henry, you have taught me well. You've shown me the path to righteousness. I feel God has a very special place for you, as you only kill to protect those who would be killed. I am sure the heavens will glow more brightly, with a halo above that massive bald head."

A big smile forms as a big hand knocks Robert forward from behind, "Let's hope so, I shall polish my head a bit more, just in case."

The two find a few seconds of laughter as they watch the masses gather and gather, like locusts upon a field of wheat.

The drums keep pounding as the sun hits mid-day. It was the old woman who came to Robert in search of an answer, "Robert Goldheart, have thou seen the older Gaelic man?"

Robert looks into the once harsh face now showing concern, "Agnes, I ... I mean, Agnes of Old, I have not seen Mica this day. No one has passed out these gates, but I wonder ..." Robert feels compassion, "Agnes of Old, I am sure Mica is no fool, as you do not grow old by being a fool." For the first time, Agnes looks as if she is in need of a caring pair of arms, and is given a hug by the Knight.

A sudden *thump* turns them around. "Sir Knight, I ask you unhand my lady. I am gone just a few hours infiltrating those here to destroy us, and come back to find this beautiful lady in your arms!"

Robert almost has to smile as he lets Agnes go.

As Agnes approaches Mica, a sudden loud, "**Whack!**" echoes throughout the castle as the older gent has a patch of red forming on the side of his face.

With a stern finger in his face, "You shall never frighten nor worry me again! What are you thinking? You are no longer a climbing majestic ram, but an old loveable goat!"

Now Robert is laughing as he watches a sight he thought he would never see, Agnes, kissing a welt she had produced.

"Come my Mica, I shall put cool waters and care on that bruise." Mica smiles, as he knows Agnes of Old cares for him.

Sending her ahead, Mica looks at Robert, "Prepare for the middle of darkness. They will light fires, but most will be within striking distance of the castle."   With Mica's news, many take time to rest and not worry about the distant sound of repetitive thunder.

While an old woman is treating the old stricken face, a short haired Lady approaches the Knight on watch. "Robert, you have not slept in a day's time. If these demons come tonight, you must be at your best. Come rest, there are many on alert if needed. My chamber is no longer being watched, as my chaperone now has duties of her own. Come, my husband to be, as I wish to show you how much I am in love with you."

As two hands interlock, what was once thought lost is now forever bound. Both hearts know this may be so special a moment of love they share, that God Himself may forgive them.

At the same time, an old couple feels a loving touch that they had thought they could never feel again. Many couples will spend a few moments of love, some will become sweet memories, and for some, it will be their last moment of bliss.

PART 24

The sun soon bade its farewell, and the coming darkness will bid many a soul the same.

Those inside the walls hear the massive drumming stop; and a dead silence comes forth from the night. The Knights observing from above can make out in the distance, a slow moving tide upon the ground moving their way.

Giving the signal for all to make ready with their bows with the special arrows, Robert takes a deep breath, "Light them, and fire!!!"

The black skies instantly light up as a volley of arrows, each ablaze, is sent out. As some strike the ground surrounding the castle, others hit their mark setting a screaming Norse afire. Seeing the massive horde with climbing ladders, another round of flames is sent skyward, as thousands charge.

Týr motions others to prepare for his plan, but will it be enough to save this night?

Those with bows are now launching arrow after arrow into the skies, while those on the ground below, receive this hail of death and begin to fall.

In the enemy camp, the agonizing cries are heard, and Víðarr smiles, "Well my commanders, that sound means more profit for us. Soon thousands will be upon the walls scaling over, and then I will take what should have been mine, and enjoy the King's cousin."

Looking at the walls in the distance, the glow of apparent small flames sends no alarms, Víðarr just smiles thinking, "It appears some are about to get a very hot bath, what a cleansing death. But then those inside will die within the filth of their bloody bowels!"

With the first groups of ladders hitting the walls, Týr gives the signal to pour the secret warmed substance into the newly created clay channels above the castle walls. Openings in the wall allow the warm liquid to flow down upon those preparing to climb up. The sound of Norse battle cries fill the ears of those inside. Just as a few reach the upper walls, Týr gives the last signal, and the warm fluids which have run down around the castle, are lit. Within a few seconds, the attackers are caught in an inferno with no escape. The dry foliage around the walls is set ablaze as well. The yells of battle are replaced by screams of agony and terror, as the fires begin to burn hotter and hotter, and burning flesh is dropping from the ladders of death.

The bowmen from above brave the flames and intense heat and start to pick off those still approaching, bringing the horde to a horrified halt.

Víðarr, watching from his vantage point, sees the skies around the castle turn from night to day. Seeing and hearing the burning death before him, he turns angrily to one of his men, "Blast the horns!!! Call them back before I run you through! Damn that Týr! He has cost me too many, now I must ... yes, that I shall do!"

The Nordic horns blow, giving the attackers a sigh of relief. Those inside and above, bow their heads in thanks, as those outside and below, are surrounded by screams, death, and the stench of burnt flesh. The night had taken forty of the castles defenders, including four of Robert's Knights. Henry, Robert and even Mica had a few cuts, but no one can imagine the devastation which lies outside the walls. Having waited for just the right time for the oils and animal fats to be poured and ignited, and with the archers volley after volley, Víðarr had lost a third of his men to death or severe injury.

The morning light brings the sight of the blackened stone walls, with smoldering charred bodies still within the embers. Týr knows that some of the Norse must have gone against Víðarr's orders, as he sees a few bodies with the marks of a blade through the neck, giving a pain stricken soul, the relief of death. Something he know Víðarr cares nothing about.

The horizon shows motion, yet nothing like the day before. Robert and Henry also notice men, but not hills of them.

Týr keeps the fires around the castle lit; no, there is no more oil to set ablaze, but Víðarr knows this not. A gut feeling, tells the three that things have changed.

An older gent, still healing from the nights wounds, once again appears out of nowhere. "They have maybe a thousand left around us, the other twelve thousand, have moved toward your King. But there is another group landing upon the shores within a day. After that, this place will be no more. And if the forces of Víðarr unite once the King's Knights and men are destroyed ... even with what Ronan brings from the north and the Normans bring from the south, this land will become the blood soaked land of Víðarr. Now, if you excuse me, I must return to my bed before Agnes the Beauty, finds me not there."

PART 25

Robert, Henry, and Týr all know it is just a matter of time as none expected more attackers from the sea.

Robert thinks for a second, and then looks at the other two, "Týr you must defend this castle at all costs and protect all those within, including what I hold dearest. Henry! The King knows you from days of old; you must make it to him, before it's too late. Edward and the Bishop look for their own glory, not knowing of the massive force that is coming, and they will end up in their graves as well. And I … I must try to slow down or halt the next wave of Víðarr's killing force. If we can make these new invaders believe that Víðarr and his first group were destroyed, they may just load back up on their ships, never to return. Then Víðarr and his force will be trapped between two forces."

"Something that worked once, perhaps will work again. Make ready, for we must leave within a very short time if we are to save all we love."

With Lady Chastity, Lady Anne, and Agnes of Old gathered, the details are revealed to them. The only change is Mica will ride with Robert as he insists he can find Ronan, and then perhaps they'll have a force follow him to the coast to assist Robert. Henry too will have another with him … the young man, who will help him through the woods, and find the quickest way to the King. Týr will have to try to keep the thousand attackers around, and make them think that he has plenty of oil, arrows and men. The plan is to have as many of the women dress in soldier's clothes, and stand or walk the walls to observing eyes. All know deception, is what will keep them alive and the English crown.

And so again, Lady Chastity and Agnes of Old as well as Lady Anne must bid farewell to men they so respect and love.

Robert looks into the beautiful eyes before him, "I love you, and have loved you from first sight. I shall always love you, this world and the next."

Robert continues, "I give you back this half of what we were once given by that wonderful Agnes of Old. We shall reclaim them upon my return as then, we shall be as one for eternity. God brought you to me, and me to you, and my love for you, within my soul, shall never die."

Their lips meet tenderly and both fear that this might be their last kiss. Lady Chastity gives her Knight a blue ribbon of velvet, tying it in a circle and placing it over Robert's head, "This is a good luck symbol and a token of my never ending love for you Robert; I shall pray that I am back within your loving arms soon." A final few seconds of loving passion is exchanged, before two must part again for the unknown.

Off to the side, an old couple look lovingly at each other. Gently grabbing the time weathered cheeks before her, "You best return to me Mica, for if not, I shall kill you myself." And then a kiss …

As they prepare to leave, Robert looks at Lady Anne, "Forgive me my Lady for I need pause on my vow to you. But know those I have sent to gather the Norman's, are entrusted with my sacred vow. They should arrive and be here for your safety."

Lady Anne looks at Chastity, "May I?" With an approving nod, Lady Anne places a kiss on a Knight's cheek, as she thinks of another she had done the same once so long ago.

Lady Anne had been clever enough to grab the seal of the husband that left her for dead, and quickly writes two documents, one for Henry and one for Rolf in case they are spotted by Edward's treacherous forces. It states they are in the service of Lord Bernard. The second document is for the King himself, telling him of the conspiracies against the crown.

With night once again approaching, Henry, led by Rolf, shall ride west toward the King. After reaching an area outside the Norse boundaries, they shall start a commotion, bringing the forces their way.

Robert, Mica and twenty five others ride east toward the coast, with every possible English flag banner along with them.

High above, a Lady can see them ride off, as well as notice that the old woman next to her is welling up with tears.

Agnes takes Chastity's hand, "I have not felt like this since I was your age. It is a wonderful feeling to have when your love is close by, but brings an aching heart when it wanders afar."

The two see Lady Anne standing alone and make their way to gather her into their hearts, as she looks **over the horizon** , still feeling the pain of years gone by.

PART 26

Laying in his goose down bed, the Bishop looks at the woman dressing, "This was our last meeting. You shall never come to me again, for soon, I shall be in Rome and in the arms of many Italian wenches."

Shocked, and hurt, the lady softly replies, "But you have said many a time that I was special. That I was the only one that ever caught the eye of a man of God such as you. I have told you the secrets that the Queen has shared with me."

The Bishop smirks, "Yes, you were special ... a special flower which I was happy to be the first to pluck. You were at times like a special dessert, which I looked forward to tasting. But when you were most special, was when you were confiding in me and sharing the Royal secrets."

"Your special confessions gave me inside information on the King and Queen. Now go! If ever you speak of us, be assured you will be burned at the stake as a witch! Now leave, and never look upon me again!!!"

The young lass rushes out in tears and in fear of her life, while a Bishop folds his hands behind his head and lays back upon the feathery pillow, "Ahhhh Rome ... I can already feel the power, and see those curvy young Italian signorinas."

PART 27

Moving westward, Henry and Rolf have passed Víðarr and his forces, and have also passed through the lines of those loyal to Edward. If all goes well, they shall make it to the King, a day and a half before the conquering force can strike.

While in the east, Mica has brought Robert and the group to the hills overlooking the shore where the next Norse invaders will come ashore. Seeing a bright fire on the beach and a few men gathered, they know that this is the place.

The first thing to do is rid the beach of the awaiting Norse greeting party. Then to keep the fires going so the force lands there and finally put their plans into action.

With Pegasus in full stride, the powerful legs run through the half dozen Norse, who are quickly mowed down by Robert and four Knights. Watching the eastern waters where they would soon be coming, the Knights bury the dead and settle onto the higher ground above. Dividing up into pairs, the group spreads out to place banners. Soon the top of the hills were ablaze with banners of all kinds, blowing their markings in the wind. Each man also made two fires, fifty paces apart. To anyone approaching shore, it would appear as if a massive force was awaiting them. This will buy time, as the invaders will wait for their fleet before storming the beaches.

Mica had ridden off toward the north to ask Ronan for reinforcements.

Now it was just time that was needed.

PART 28

Back at the castle, Týr and a few men now walk the walls as some of the women take a nightly break.

Darkness falls and the fires of those wishing to take the castle start to flicker in the distance. They hopefully just need to hold out one more day, then those from the northwest or southwest, should arrive, sending the evil invaders eastward to report to Víðarr.

Walking a few more steps, Týr sees a rope and a clawed iron upon the ground, neatly rolled up. Wanting to call an alarm, he hesitates, as he looks at the rope. Rubbing his beard, "Okay ... why would one of Víðarr's men scale a wall, not kill a soul, or even try to open the gate to let the others in? Something is odd here."

Picking up the rope and bringing it into the light, Týr can tell that this rope is not one from the Norse outside. Bringing his torch toward the wall, two sets of footsteps coated with the ashes of the dead can clearly be seen.

Týr quickly drops the rope and runs toward the Lady's and Agnes's sleeping quarters.

Quickly and silently walking into the Lady's chamber, Týr sees the three on the terrace in conversation. Slowly scouring the room, he sees nothing. Then, as Lady Anne turns to walk back in, the shine from behind a tapestry reveals what Týr searches for. Unsheathing his blade, Týr rushes toward the wall hanging as Anne is about to enter, yelling, "STOP!"

The Lady halts as a face appears only to have a blade pierce through the fabric, and into the assailant's chest. Looking into the mortally wounded man's eyes, Týr yells, "Who sent you! And where is the other? Tell me and I shall end the pain that is upon you. Quickly!"

The man's mouth is already filling with blood, "I say nothing ... but Lord Bernard sends his regards."

Týr pulls out the blade, then instantly thrusts it into the man's heart.

Agnes and Chastity have now rushed over to the commotion. Anne instinctively walks back out toward them, as the Old Norse voice yells, "**NO!**"

Týr rushes toward Anne. In the blink of an eye, Týr is between Anne and the other tower just as an arrow strikes the once Norse leader, who drops his blade. Seeing the women starting to huddle, a figure is quickly running across the narrow castle wall between the two towers with blade in hand. Picking up her father's blade, just as the man is almost upon them, Chastity hurls the blade, striking the man in his chest and he falls off toward the burnt corpses below.

Anne looks at Chastity, "By the hand of God your blade flew to its mark. Chastity, you saved us all, as this was another sent by my former husband to slay me."

Chastity rushes toward her father as she looks toward Anne, "That was not God's doing, that was my fathers! He trained me well."

Having watched what his daughter had done from where he lays Týr looks at her and smiles, "Yes … just as I taught you. If your brother and mother would have lived, they would have both been so proud. You are so strong my daughter you have never shown fear, sorrow yes … but never fear. Now comes the time, you must show neither. Having fought many battles in my day, I know where this arrow lies, and my time is short. I ask you to feel no sorrow, as I will again be with your mother and brother in a place called Heaven. I ask but one thing, give me a Norse funeral with the fire of fires for all to see, and include this man called Jesus whom I shall soon stand before."

"Lady Anne you are safe...Agnes, thank you my dearest ..."

Týrs eyes now close as three sets of eyes fill with tears and an old voice whispers, "It's Agnes of Old, my old dear friend."

In the attire of a Norse soldier, with sparkling eyes and blond hair, now growing a bit longer, Chastity lights the kindling below the massive wood framed platform high up on a tower. The tower faces eastward toward the land of the Norseman's birth. The flames start to come alive within the early morning darkness, lighting the sky as if a new day was rising. When news of their leader's heroic death reached the masses, his last wishes were in place in short time.

Taking command, Lady Chastity, is now the leader of the Christians from their former land of the Norse.

Some of the attackers outside the castle rise and watch, as many remember tribute fires for fallen leaders within their clans. Many began to question their own honor as it is paid for and distributed by a few pieces of Víðarr's silver.

PART 29

A knock at the estates door is quickly answered, "Hurry, come in ... Lord Edward awaits you."

A figure, awkwardly walking, dressed in English attire, is escorted before Edward. "Víðarr wishes to meet with you, the Bishop, and the rest who financed this crown for you. He wishes to know that if for a percentage, you will back him in the taking of France, the Normans, and the Germans. He will return to you, twenty percent of all gold and silver. All you need to do is not come to their aid. But, being a man of honor, Víðarr must see it in your eyes to see if your words are true. Bring as many military escorts as you please, as we have an accord."

Before daylight, the conference begins in a large tent, just a few hours march from the King's palace. Edward walks toward Víðarr, "So you are the great one that I have heard so much about. Welcome! I hope our silver and riches have served you and your hired men well."

Víðarr stares at Edward, the Bishop, Bernard and a handful of other Lords. Looking each one up and down, "Well, I am pleased you came, even with the number of men you brought to protect you. They are being given food and drink as we speak." Looking at the Bishop, Víðarr smiles, "Oh and you must be the Bishop; I hear you will soon be Pope of this Christian belief. Will you give me ten percent of the churches riches?"

The Bishop thinks for a second, "That I am afraid I cannot do, perhaps one or two percent?"

Víðarr smiles, "You are as much of a so called Christian as I."

Walking up to a few of the other supporters of Edward, Víðarr swiftly pulls out a blade in each hand and slicing two of their throats, then looks at the Bishop, "Ten percent?"

Suddenly all those gathered, wish to leave. Edward smiles, "Well that certainly raises the percentage for you."

Víðarr now smiles, "So you say, if all are no longer alive, except for you and the Bishop … then it would be ten percent?"

Edward with his pompous smile starts to laugh, "Well yes, it's all about the wealth isn't it? Then you get the power." Edward quickly raises a dagger and sticks it into Bernard's throat. Looking at Víðarr for approval, "He was married to the King's cousin."

Now the wolves have turned upon their own kind. Víðarr stares at the Bishop, as the rest of the English financiers are run through, "Fifteen percent if I get England?"

Now the Bishop fears for his life, "Yes ... yes. I give you my word as next Pope."

Now Víðarr has turned the hopeful Pope to be, against the hopeful King to be.

Edward wants to call for his guards but knows if he does, he will be dead before their arrival. He doesn't yet know that all of his security men have already been disposed of.

Víðarr can see daylight is approaching as the morning light filters in through the opening of the tent. He summons his commanders to enjoy a bit of morning sport. Looking at the porky Bishop, and the thin framed Edward, Víðarr smiles as he tosses two swords to the ground, "Wait until I say to begin; then you will pick up the swords! The one who slays the other ... lives."

Laughter fills the tent as men begin to wager which one of these pathetic looking men will win. After a few moments all bets have been made, and Víðarr claps his hands loudly, "Begin!"

Those in attendance begin to laugh as both combatants struggle even to pick up their weapons. All can tell that these two have not so as much as slain a chicken. The groans and the misses as both try to survive have the men yelling for the one they put wages on. Finally, the Bishop loses his balance and falls backwards, Edward approaches for a final blow standing over his former friend, and looking back at Víðarr with a sly grin. Meanwhile, the Bishop musters all his might and lifts his blade upward, right into the groin of Edward. The would-be King's eyes bulge out as the tent is filled with cheers and laughter. Pieces of silver pass between Norse hands, as the shocked Bishop pulls his blade out in horror, and watches Edward fall to the ground, with his 'manhood' no longer intact.

Struggling, the Bishop now stands over his friend, "Goodbye Edward". As the sword is thrust forward into the dying man's throat, it brings more cheers as a plume of blood sprays skyward.

Breathing heavily, the Bishop looks at Víðarr, "Fifteen percent when I am Pope".

Víðarr smiles and walks over to the supposed Christian Holy man, "Yes ... I will have use for you. For, I am taking ALL of England for myself. Thanks to those who have paid for these men, and thousands more that soon arrive ... perhaps even as we speak. I had no plans of taking Rome and the Vatican, but now I realize there is enormous wealth within it. And *you* my Bishop shall deliver it to me. For after this day, if those around you either near or far, find out what you have done, they will certainly burn you alive. A bit painful I guarantee you."

PART 30

Robert and his small group of men watch as the distant sea brings forth many sails. Getting closer to shore, they slow, and take notice. Seeing the many groups of English banners waving in the cool channel winds; it appears as if thousands of men are waiting for their arrival, and a battle. Skegar, bastard son of Víðarr, signals a few vessels to move next to his.

Robert can see that the leaders of these Norsemen are in conference. Smiling slightly, the Knight's thoughts are, "The longer you stay there, the more time we have to save England, and the King. Hurry Mica, hurry you old sly Gaelic."

With the sounds of the waves below and the gulls up high, the peaceful sounds are abruptly replaced by a loud roar as the Norsemen begin to row forward with great speed. Now Robert must ready his few, and instruct the rest.

Quickly gathering the group, "My loyal friends … our deception has lasted only a short time. They come, and I, along with my four Knights will welcome them to English ground, and buy as much time as possible. The rest of you have been introduced to the long bow. With your steeds, you can fire a volley and be well out of harm's way quickly. Do this often. You too must buy time. I pray that Henry got through in time, and that the Normans have landed, and are heading toward all those you and I hold dear. But most of all, I pray that a feisty old Gael arrives in time with his countrymen. Fight hard and die well." Robert now looks at the four Knights, "Make ready, we will take many Norsemen! They will never see more than the shores of England."

All five know, this will be their last hour, unless a miracle comes to pass.

Walking to his old four legged friend, Robert strokes his long face softly, "Well Pegasus, I am afraid this may be our last fight in this world." I could have never had a better steed than thou.

"Ride hard, and let us both ride off into English legend."

Mounting up, the Knights grab their lances and ride toward a hill overlooking the approaching invaders. The rest, on horseback, divide into two groups; one on each side of the invading foes, ready to fire volley upon volley of arrows to kill as many as they can, before they ride back to defend the small castle.

The first Norse ships come to a stop in the waist high waters, sending hordes of men over the sides and toward the beach. Robert stops at a nearby tree, placing an object upon it, he whispers, "I'm sorry my love, please forgive me. You will be of my last thought on earth, and my first thought within heaven."

The signal is given and five of the bravest men in all of England charge forward to their destiny.

The first group of invaders reach the sinking sands of the beach and are quickly run through, some two at a time, with the sharpened points of a charging Knight's lance. The Englishmen upon their battle trained horses are moving at a great speed, much faster than their adversaries ever thought. The incoming tides are soon turning red with the flow of Norse blood. The loyal Christian Norse on the hill fire off their volleys, then ride off to make ready, knowing too soon, the Knights will be greatly overwhelmed.

PART 31

Setting the Bishop upon a horse, Víðarr looks into the clearly frightened eyes, "You tell the rest of those who are blinded by power that those you came with will arrive shortly. We shall march when the sun is highest, and be upon the unsuspecting before it sets. And Bishop, if you betray me, I shall slowly cut you open from your groin to your fat lined throat."

Hitting the horse on the rump, the Bishop is quickly off, sweating heavily with relief. He is no more than over the next hill when he is knocked off his horse and is out of breath on the ground, dazed and lightheaded.

Without notice a pair of large hands lifts the overweight clergy up by his throat, "You so much as cough and I shall rip off your blasphemous head and soil upon your innards."

Looking up, the Bishop sees the angry face of Henry the Bald. The Bishop's face is brought closer to Henry's as he whispers, "Are they just over the ridge? No words; just shake your head, yes, or no."

The terrified clergyman nervously moves his head up and down.

"Is Víðarr among them and will they be moving this way?" Again the Bishop acknowledges.

Henry pushes the round man up to a tree. Looking at him with fire in his eyes, "I should send you to the hell that awaits you now. But I'm sure that the King and Rome have other plans for you. Remove your robe, and make not even a squeak!"

Within minutes, the half-dressed Bishop is securely bound to a tree, with his under garments shoved into his mouth to keep him quiet. Henry pulls his massive sword and swings it; striking the tree just a hair above the Bishop's shaking head. Henry growls, "If you are not here when I return, I shall find you and happily cut you in two!"

PART 32

Lady Chastity and Lady Anne now walk the walls along with other women dressed as soldiers, giving those outside the castle the illusion of many fighting men that are ready for battle.

It is almost the middle of the day when a distant commotion is heard. Chastity sees a trail of dust swiftly approaching the castle. As they get closer, she can see that these men on horseback are battle Knights. Nearly two hundred strong, these riders cut their way through the southern force of the Norse, and head toward the castle. With a clear and commanding voice, Chastity yells, "Open the gates! The Norman's have arrived!"

A sigh of relief is heard within the castle walls as Knight after Knight ride through the gates, and into the courtyard.

Chastity hurries down from the tower as she recognizes two of the Knights, who were part of Robert and Henry's group. Lady Anne hurries to catch up to Chastity, stopping just short of those gathered around applauding these Normans.

Then a face with long gray locks catches the King's cousin's eye; her heart begins to pound in her chest as she takes another look.

Still dressed as a soldier, Lady Anne rushes over and yells, "Franz! Franz Zieboltz! Over here!"

A man almost as big as Henry the Bald, looks over and sees what appears to be a soldier screaming with a beautiful voice. A voice he has not heard in many a year. Focusing, the German Knights eyes see the impossible! His large heart also begins to also pound. "Lady Anne! Is it truly you?"

As the Lady nods of her head yes, the Knight leaps off his steed and they rush toward each other.

With one big swoop, his arms are once again filled with what both had thought was just a loving memory.

Agnes of Old comes along and stands at the side of Chastity, bearing a smile that has rarely been seen. "And so one is back with the love she has never forgotten. May we soon also be blessed with such a divine reunion"

PART 33

While the seas waves still run red, Skegar leads his horde up the beach and over the hills. Large columns of wicked Norsemen follow their leader. As they swiftly march along, a man nearest to Skegar suddenly buckles over with an arrow protruding through his neck. Then another, and yet another!

Soon many men are being struck down by arrows, as others instinctively raise their shields for protection. Peering out, Skegar can see small groups of horsemen on either side of his men, firing arrow after arrow. Giving a signal, Skegar has hundreds of men break from the north and south of his line and charge the men in great numbers. The men on horseback do as Robert had instructed. They disperse and ride ahead for another suitable place for an ambush.

The evil masses didn't have to wait long, as again, death from above begins to take more Norse souls. Having started with many quivers of arrows, the horsemen are now down to their last ones. It appears that now, they too must prepare for a final stand, and take as many invaders with them as they can to the beyond.

Skegar gives his men the, "Shields up!" signal, knowing this is not a good tactical place to be.

As the last arrows fly, most of the men that are hit have wounds to their lower extremities.

Now completely out of ammunition, one of Týrs men looks across to the other side, and raises his sword to signal a charge down the hill and into this valley of death! About to lower his sword, a loud blaring of horns fills the valley from above them. Looking back, the men on horseback can clearly see the Gaels, with their leader Ronan. Within seconds, Ronan's men send a barrage of lethal projectiles which descend upon the now dying hordes of invaders.

Skegar, bastard son of Víðarr, signals for a retreat back to the shore. He's sure that his father must have failed, and soon all of the English and those from the north will finish him as well. The masses are soon scrambling to the safety of their vessels. The few that were left behind to guard the ships stand and watch in disbelief. In short time, the vessels are boarded, missing many a Norseman. Skegar now proclaims he is the leader of all the Norse, as his father must surely be dead.

PART 34

Having surveyed an open field not far from the King's palace, Víðarr's men have reassured their leader, that their surprise attack will be even easier than all thought. With watchful cautious eyes, Víðarr leads his men across the open field. Making it about half way with still no sign of alarm, Víðarr stops his invaders. Looking forward, then back and then side to side, the warrior becomes alarmed; as this is the worst possible place to be caught in, yet, there they are.

A spooked flock of birds from a wooded area brings Víðarr's mind to a quick decision, "Back! Back! We must hurry back!"

Before his men can turn, the sunlight turns to darkness, with thousands of arrows in flight.

Víðarr has led his men into a trap! Looking back from whence they came, there soon appears a massive line of men on horseback, with lances raised high and the shine of steel reflecting their deadly points. Looking forward, Víðarr sees the same. With man after man falling from the bowmen on the sides, the Norsemen are like fish in a barrel. Raising his sword the defiant Norse leader yells, "All eastward and to the shores! Kill as many as you can along the way!"

Víðarr's thousands now rush in retreat, while a line of Knights make ready for their approach. They shall ride toward those heading for them. The Knights behind them will wait until those with lances have cleared; then they will also attack ... coming from behind the fleeing invaders from beyond the sea.

The massive man and the boy named Rolf, son of the woodsman Han, had made it in time to warn the King, and save the crown and the Isles.

Víðarr has made it past the oncoming forces as he dashes closer to the cover of the woods.

Just about to enter, a massive man with a bald head appears. His horse, which matches his size, is given a kick and moves forward.

Víðarr's eyes widen, then turn to hate, as he pulls his sword to strike at the legs of the massive steed. The leader of the Norse ducks low, preparing to strike, but the well skilled Knight has seen this maneuver many a time. Both Knight and horse make an abrupt move and a lance is stuck straight down into the would-be assailant's spine, pinning him to the ground. Víðarr's body goes numb.

Dismounting, the large Knight walks over to look into the eyes of the evil dying man.

Only able to move his eyes, Víðarr struggles to speak, "You may have won this day ... but from what a Bishop has told me ... Edward and his half-brother ... your 'son' Robert ... live no more."

Víðarr starts to cough and laugh at the same time, "You did not know? I see it in your face!"

Deep within his heart and mind, Henry *does* know the words spoken are true, as he has always had a special bond with Robert, and an everlasting love for his mother. A fatherly love that has unknowingly always been there suddenly turns into a feeling of panic. Rushing back to his steed, Henry prepares to ride off eastward as fast as his four legged friend can go. Riding away, the ears of the Bald ignore the words that become fainter as he rides, Víðarr's harsh voice echo out,

"Finish me off, father of the bastard!"

Many of the paid mercenaries now lie dead or wounded, as a bald head and his steed ride past.

Henry thinks of all the times that he and Robert had shared since Roberts mother, Bernadette's passing. He thinks of all the years of loving the woman he could never have, and of the love that she only had for him. It all races through his large bald head. To finally find out what his heart has always tried to tell him, is now a weight that lies heavily within the giant of Knight's heart.

PART 35

The Norman Knights and one prestigious German Knight watch from the castle as the Norse are quickly moving eastward, toward a fleet of ships they hope will still be there. They do not know that they will soon run into Gaelic warriors. Most who followed Víðarr now lay dead or wounded. Very few will make it aboard the last ships that sail eastward...never to return.

The King with his Knights at his side, now ride through the land and come upon the dead noblemen who had conspired against him; those that Víðarr had slain.

Seeing Lord Edward and Bernard among them, the King speaks, "They will stay where they lay, let the beasts of the forest feed upon these treacherous vermin!"

As they head back toward the palace, movement is spotted, and the King and his Knights alertly stop. Looking toward a wooded area, the King sees the Bishop tied and gagged to a tree. As one of his Knights is about to go help the man, the King raises his hand to stop him. All now see a pair of large boars circling the terrified Bishop. As the King and the Bishop make eye contact, the King lowers his hand, "Nothing to see here, for swine shall feast upon swine."

As they turn to ride away, a well fed Bishop's lower body begins to be violently torn apart and eaten by the beasts with the gleaming white tusks.

PART 36

Reaching the castle of Týr, Henry's steed has served him well, and is in great need of rest. Seeing two of his fellow Knights, a brief reunion is in order as Henry just has time for water and another steed, so he can begin his rush to the coast. Lady Chastity, Lady Anne, and an old familiar face from long ago are also present. Getting a brief smile upon his face, "I see my favorite German Knight has aged well."

Franz smiles back, "As have you; my big bald headed English friend."

Looking into Henry's eyes, Franz already knows, "I have men at the ready, we go with you to the coast to seek your Knight Robert. But I see that you already know he is more than that."

Henry is a bit shocked, "How may you know this?"

Lady Anne steps forward now, as now Agnes has also joined the mix, "Lady Bernadette told me of this long ago, but I was sworn to secrecy."

Chastity is now also readying a horse, as the Henry looks her way, "And where may the Lady be riding off to?"

With eyes of fire she looks back at the large bald man, "With you! In search of your son, and my soon to be husband! My father's death has made me the leader of my people ... Do not even try to stop me!"

About to mount up, a voice calls out, "May I too have a steed and a quick bite to take with me, and I can show you the fastest way."

Agnes's worries are now comforted, as what she also holds dear is standing right before her. Handing Mica a jug and a leather bag full of food, "I was already prepared for your arrival. Upon your return Mica the Gael, you may never wander again from my eyes, until God wishes it so."

In a few moments the group is off, stopping just long enough to thank Ronan for his support. He is also given a promise of friendship by Henry, as those are the wishes of a grateful King.

Agnes and Lady Anne stand together as they watch and pray once more, that who they so hold dear, will return again safely. Agnes's eyes look into Lady Anne's, ... both know what they have once again found, may be forever lost to a Lady of the Norse.

Approaching the coast, the Knights, Lady Chastity and their old guide begin to come across the carnage of war. Many Norse cover the grounds along the way. All eyes are looking for any type of miraculous movement, revealing perhaps a wounded Knight. Reaching the shore, the groups of once planted banners blow softly in the winds, with the sound of squawking gulls filling air while feeding upon the dead.

Henry looks at a horrified Lady Chastity, "You stay here with Mica, what lies upon the beaches should never be embedded within your mind. If I find him among the dead, I shall make my son as presentable as I can."

Chastity nervously watches as Franz and Henry along with the others, walk among the dead. One by one, the men Robert rode with are found and gently set aside. But there is no sign of a son or a husband to be. The wind starts to pick up, and Chastity's eyes catch a glimpse of something.

Running as fast as she can ... as she gets closer, she already knows what it is. Stopping before it, she tenderly reaches out and takes the item in her hands. It is the other half of what she wears under her garments ... half of a golden heart on a blue velvet ribbon. Softly touching the loving object, the tears begin to flow from the beautiful eyes.

The sounds of movement behind her startle the Lady, as she quickly turns.

Having to look twice, she sees Pegasus making his way toward her. Discovering that the noble steed has a wound, Chastity yells down to those on the beach.

Within moments, Henry is at her side, "He has wounds, but he has had worse; he will survive. We have searched far and wide, only the four who rode with Robert have been found. We shall search some more …."

PART 37

Henry and two loyal Knights wave farewell as they leave the castle of Lady Chastity of the Norse. At her side stands Agnes of Old, and what shall have her heart the rest of her days, Mica.
Lady Anne also watches within the secure arms of who she so long ago dreamed of. The King has granted all properties once held by Bernard, to his cousin, and soon to be German husband, Knight Zieboltz. All watch and pray that what Henry the Bald, goes in search of, will safely be found.

Tales of the Knights

Volume 1

Over the Horizon

Epilogue

The warm summer days have turned into the frosts of winter as a now long haired Lady rides out of the castle on a majestic white steed.

Riding to the same point that she has visited since the day of the bald man's departure, she looks to the east from on top of a hill. Her hands grasp the two hearts that are now joined together as one, on a single blue velvet ribbon.

"God, it is I again ... I have come for my daily prayers. I vowed to give you thanks each and every day, and I again humbly ask for either a sign of hope or even closure. I feel in my heart that Robert is someone who *is* ... not someone who was. Please look after Henry the Bald and those with him. I pray You bring his son home before the day that You shall call us all into Your House."

She bows her head, and the steed does the same.

Both heads slowly rise, and look toward the suns glorious golden rays as they rise,

> ... ***over the horizon***.

Stay tuned for

TALES OF THE KNIGHTS 2

SINS OF THE PAST

Another Great Book from:

Diamond / DiAngelo

MUSIC AND BOOKS

Also Check Out Bobby and Rodney's Music:

Search for
"OH NO IT'S CHERRY BOMB"

Streaming on your favorite music service
WORLDWIDE

AS ALWAYS,

THANK YOU FOR SPENDING TIME WITH US, AND
READING THIS EXCITING STORY.

WE SINCERELY HOPE THAT YOU'VE ENJOYED THE
BOOK!

H.P. GOLDING AND
R.H. BAUDERER

BOBBY DIAMOND AND
RODNEY DIANGELO

TALES OF THE KNIGHTS
1

OVER THE HORIZON
REVISED EDITION

©2024

Made in the USA
Monee, IL
24 April 2024

57346650R00118